One of the funniest authors for children, Jeanne Willis has been writing since she was five and is the author of many children's books including *Tadpole's Promise*, *Who's in the Loo*, *Bottoms Up* and the hugely popular *Dr Xargle* series.

She has won numerous awards including the Smarties Prize, the Red House Children's Book Award and the Sheffield Children's Book Award.

An enormously popular cartoonist and illustrator, Arthur Robins has illustrated bestselling books by Laurence Anholt, Martin Waddell and Michael Rosen, including *Little Rabbit Foo Foo*, and has even produced some stamps for the Royal Mail.

Available in the
Downtown Dinosaurs series:

Dinosaur Olympics
Dinosaurs in Disguise
Dinosaur Scramble

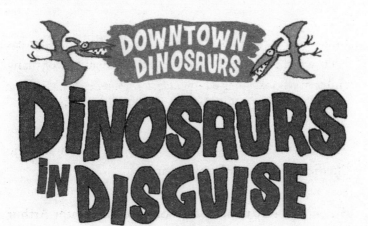

DOWNTOWN DINOSAURS
DINOSAURS IN DISGUISE

JEANNE WILLIS

Illustrated by Arthur Robins

Piccadilly Press • London

For Andrea Reece, with thanks
J. W.

For Susanna, from the old dinosaur
A.R.

First published in Great Britain in 2012
by Piccadilly Press Ltd,
5 Castle Road, London NW1 8PR
www.piccadillypress.co.uk

Text copyright © Jeanne Willis, 2012
Illustrations copyright © Arthur Robins, 2012

A catalogue record for this book is available
from the British Library

ISBN: 978 1 84812 268 0

3 5 7 9 10 8 6 4 2

Printed in the UK by CPI (UK) Group, Ltd, Croydon, CR0 4YY
Cover design by Simon Davis
Cover illustration by Arthur Robins

CHAPTER 1

A JURASSIC CLASSIC

There was a terrible kerfuffle going on in Fossil Street. Judging by the swearing and screaming coming from the Stigsons' house, anyone would have thought that the Downtown carnivores had returned to knock the stuffing out of the peace-loving Uptown herbivores again.

However, it was worse than that. Uncle Loops had lost his cap. Like him, it was extremely old and battered but it was his favourite and, because he wouldn't shut up until he found it, the whole family was forced to search the house from top to bottom.

'It's a Jurassic classic!' he wailed. 'They don't make them like that any more.'

'Thank goodness,' muttered Mr Stigson. 'It looked like a cow pat.' Mrs Stigson stopped searching behind the cushions and glared at him.

'Maurice, don't be unkind – he'll hear you.'

'No, I won't!' bellowed Loops. 'My hearing aid was in my cap. I've lost that too!'

His young nephew Darwin took him aside and whispered kindly in his ear. 'You've still got it on, Uncle.'

Loops gave a wrinkly smile as he felt around on top of his scaly head. 'I still have my cap on?'

'No, your hearing aid.'

Uncle Loops checked in the mirror and his face fell.

'When did you have it last?' asked Darwin.

'My hearing aid?'

'Your cap,' said Darwin patiently.

'Give me strength!' grumbled Mr Stigson as he mimed strangling Uncle Loops.

Uncle Loops thought long and hard but, by then, he'd completely forgotten what he was supposed to be remembering. At one hundred and ninety years old, his recent memory wasn't as good as it used to be but, as Darwin cheerfully reminded him, all was not lost; he could still recall the Ice Age at the drop of a hat.

'That's it!' Uncle Loops beamed. 'I dropped my hat. I doffed it at Fat Phyllis next door by way of a hello and dropped it on her front step.'

Mrs Stigson winced. 'Uncle Loops, you must stop calling her Fat Phyllis. Mrs Merrick may be a bit on the flabby side, even for a mastodon, but she's a good neighbour. Please don't upset her.'

Just then the doorbell rang and before any one could stop him, Uncle Loops had pottered off on his zimmer frame to open it.

'It's Flabby Phyllis!' he announced.

The plus-sized mastodon looked down her trunk at him and snorted. 'You're all charm, aren't you, Augustus? I only came round to tell you what had happened to that dreadful old cap of yours and now I shan't bother.'

She cast her eyes over the upturned furniture, the tipped-out drawers and the lifted rug.

'Please bother,' sighed Mr Stigson wearily. 'We've hunted high and low.'

Mrs Merrick shrugged.

'I have a very large Victoria sponge cake,' pleaded Mrs Stigson, opening a tin and going straight for Phyllis's weak spot.

'Very well, but it will take more than a couple of slices to get over the hurtful name-calling, Lydia,' insisted Mrs Merrick, as she hoovered out the cream and jam filling.

'I think you misheard,' said Mrs Stigson. 'Uncle Loops has loose dentures. What he actually called you was *Fabby* Phyllis.'

The mastodon chewed it over along with most of the cake and blushed girlishly. 'Yes, I rather suspected he'd taken a bit of a fancy to me when he doffed his cap and made that funny gesture with his hand,' she simpered.

'Well, if you tell me where it is, I'll just go and get it,' said Darwin, heading out the door.

'Waste of time, dear!' called Mrs Merrick. 'You might as well come back in. You won't find it out there – it's been cap-napped.'

'*Cap*-napped?' exclaimed Mr Stigson. 'Who would want that filthy old thing?'

Mrs Merrick arched her thick, woolly eyebrows. 'Who do you honestly think took his cap? Who always plays tricks on us and steals anything that isn't bolted down?'

The Stigsons didn't have to make a wild guess. They knew exactly who the culprit was: the hairy little sub-human with opposable thumbs who had been the bane of their lives for years. When he wasn't changing their round bicycle wheels for square ones, he was switching signposts, or setting fire to things.

'The australopithecus!' they groaned in unison.

'Why would Ozzi want my cap?' bleated Uncle Loops. 'He's only got a tiny head.'

It was true. Ozzi's skull was only a fraction of the size of a stegosaurus's but the brain inside it seemed to have evolved a lot more than anyone cared to admit.

'I've a nasty feeling that australopithecus isn't as stupid as he looks,' Mr Stigson muttered darkly.

'Ozzi looked pretty stupid in that cap,' said Mrs Merrick, 'but so would anybody. I tried to snatch it back when he grabbed it off the step but that vicious pet cynognathus of his almost had my hand off.'

Pulling a knitted tea cosy over his head to keep off the chill, Uncle Loops shuffled to the

front door in his slippers.

'Where are you off to, Uncle?' asked Darwin.

'A barn dance,' said Uncle Loops.

He wasn't really. For a moment, he couldn't remember where he was going or why but when

he got to the end of the front path and skidded in

a steaming pile of cynognathus poop, it all came back to him.

'I'm going to get my cap back off that thieving little furry beggar!' he said to himself, and with that, he headed off as fast as he could – which was very slowly – in the direction of No Man's Land to confront the australopithecus.

'Uncle Loops has been gone an awfully long time,' said Mrs Stigson as she finished putting the furniture straight. 'I do hope he hasn't come to any harm.'

'He's at a barn dance, Lydia,' sighed Mr Stigson. 'What's the worst that could happen – a brachiosaurus steps on his bunion? He's survived almost two hundred years. You worry too much.'

As it turned out, Mrs Stigson had every reason to worry. Three hours later, Uncle Loops returned looking muddy and dishevelled – and appeared to be in a state of shock. The tea cosy he'd been wearing as a hat was full of leaves and the pom pom on the top had completely unravelled.

'Good grief, Augustus!' said Mrs Merrick, who had long since demolished the sponge cake and had started on the biscuit tin. 'What happened? You look as if you've been dragged through a hedge backwards.'

'Forwards,' insisted Uncle Loops.

'It must have been one heck of a barn dance,' said Mrs Stigson.

Uncle Loops, not for the first time, looked confused. 'Dance?' he said. 'I haven't been to a dance. I went to find that australopithecus and give him a piece of my mind.'

'Can't have been a very large piece,' chortled Mrs Merrick.

Darwin helped his beloved old uncle into a chair and put a blanket over his knees.

'What happened, Uncle Loops? Did you find Ozzi? Did you fight him for your cap?' It certainly looked as if Uncle Loops had been battling with something or somebody.

'Forget the cap, Dawson!' he said excitedly. 'I've been battling through the undergrowth to get a better look at the new dinosaur that's lurking round the Primeval Forest in No Man's Land.'

The Stigsons exchanged worried glances and

the room fell silent. Uncle Loops had lots of annoying habits but making up tall stories wasn't one of them.

'This dinosaur you saw, was it a herbivore like us, Uncle?' asked Darwin.

'I never asked,' said Loops, 'but it had the big claws and forelimbs of a typical fierce, meat-eating therapod, like a tyrannosaurus or a velociraptor.'

Mrs Stigson went pale and leant on her husband for support. 'It can't be a new carnivore,

can it, Maurice?' she whispered.

Mr Stigson nodded gravely. 'If Uncle's description is to be believed, I'm afraid so, Lydia. It's probably even more deadly than the Downtown Dinosaurs from Raptor Road!'

There was a sickening thump and a clatter as Mrs Stigson fainted and dropped the tea tray. It was hardly surprising – the evil tyrannosaurus rex, Flint Beastwood, and his motley crew of assorted carnivores had frequently invaded Fossil Street and terrorised the Uptown herbivores. Almost all of the neighbours had lost a close relative or friend to their Downtown appetites, and a bigger, nastier, flesh-eating monster was the last thing they needed.

'Pull yourself together, Lydia!' snapped Mrs Merrick, dousing her with a trunkful of water from the coelacanth tank to bring her out of her faint. 'This so-called new dinosaur was probably just a trick of the light. Augustus, you need your eyes tested.'

'I can see *you,* Fat Wallis,' sulked Uncle Loops, 'but then you're impossible to miss.'

Despite him insisting that he saw what he saw out in No Man's Land, Phyllis Merrick remained unconvinced and having reminded everyone that Uncle Loops couldn't even get her or Darwin's name right now, the Stigsons had to agree that the chances of him giving an accurate description of the mythical carnivore were pretty small.

'It was probably just a rabid badger, Lydia,' said Mr Stigson as Mrs Stigson put the broken tea cups back on the tray.

But Darwin wasn't so sure. He'd been on many walks across No Man's Land with Uncle Loops and he knew a rabid badger when he saw one.

'Why won't anyone believe me, Damian?'

mumbled Uncle Loops. 'It was a whopper . . . Hang on, is that an edmontonia cycling down our path?'

It was Boris the mayor and, after knocking frantically on the door, he burst in and made an announcement.

'Listen up, good folk of Fossil Street, I come bearing bad tidings.'

'Don't tell me, you've been re-elected,' groaned Mrs Merrick.

'Thank you for that vote of confidence,' said Boris, 'but you will be laughing on the other side of your face when you hear what I have to say.'

'Spit it out then, Doris!' said Uncle Loops.

Boris looked cautiously out of the window as if he was afraid that he'd been followed and lowered his voice. 'It is my solemn duty to tell you that there is a new dinosaur on the loose.'

Uncle Loops almost leapt up off the sofa. 'Told you so! Rabid badger, my backside.'

'*I'm* talking,' insisted Boris. 'This monster is more ghastly, more ferocious than any carnivore we have ever known. It has armoured scales and a massive spikey tail and . . .'

'No it doesn't,' heckled Uncle Loops.

'Oh yes it does!' said Boris. 'It has teeth like scythes and pointy spikes and —'

'Oh no it doesn't!' insisted Uncle Loops. 'Hey, is it pantomime season already?'

Mrs Merrick finished a doughnut and confronted Boris. 'The thing is, what are you going to do about it?' she said. 'If I get eaten alive

by an unknown carnivore, I shall hold you directly responsible.'

'That is why I am imposing a curfew,' explained Boris firmly. 'From now on, you are all banned from visiting No Man's Land after dark until we get the measure of this beast.'

Darwin's heart sank. 'But the carnival opens tomorrow evening on No Man's Land!' he wailed. 'I want to go to the fun fair.'

He'd watched them setting it up for days and he'd been really looking forward to seeing the floats and trying his hand at the coconut shy.

'It's not fun and it's not fair,' quipped Boris as he sped off on his bike. 'Better safe than sorry.'

But Darwin, being young and reckless, strongly disagreed. *Pah!* he thought, *I can look after myself.*

With the amusement arcade in mind, he went to empty his piggy bank.

CHAPTER 2

ROGUE CARNIVORE

Much as the residents of Fossil Street hated being told where they couldn't go during Boris's curfew, they were united in their fear of the unknown dinosaur rampaging around. It was the talk of the town and, overnight, it grew even bigger and more ferocious in their minds.

Late the next afternoon, another neighbour dropped in on the Stigsons and made things even worse. Mrs Merrick was still there, having stayed the night on the sofa, but that was more to do with falling asleep after over-eating than the fear of being eaten herself. Having swallowed her own body weight in breakfast muffins and lunchtime baps, she was now hinting loudly about the teatime buns. Mrs Stigson was beginning to think she'd never leave

when Sir Stratford Tempest turned up, all of a fluster. He was wearing heavy stage make-up and a false moustache as he was due to appear in a play at the No Man's Land Roundhouse but as soon as he opened his mouth, there was no mistaking the old triceratops.

'Darlings, I can't *believe* it!' he moaned. 'Nobody is allowed to venture out to the theatre in the evening and now my show has been cancelled! I wish I'd never mentioned the beast to Boris now. Not in such elaborate detail anyway. Thanks to his curfew, my career is in tatters.'

That caught Darwin's attention. From what Sir Tempest had just said, there was a distinct possibility that Boris had never seen the dinosaur in the flesh and that he'd put the curfew in place on the hearsay of an actor who was world famous for exaggerating everything.

'So *you* told the mayor about the dinosaur, Sir Tempest?' he asked. 'Did Boris actually witness it for himself?'

'He didn't need to, dear boy,' boomed the

triceratops with a dramatic flourish. 'As an actor, I was able to describe the monster so vividly, he could see it in his mind's eye and was all a-quiver. It had teeth like scythes and pointy spikes and —'

'Oh no it didn't!' insisted Uncle Loops.

'Oh yes it did!' bellowed Sir Tempest.

By now, Darwin wasn't sure what to believe about the rogue carnivore, but being rather more intelligent than the average stegosaurus, he reasoned that if the new dinosaur was *that* dangerous and *that* cunning, it would have eaten Uncle Loops the day before — he was easy meat — but for whatever reason, it had left him alone. With that in mind, Darwin decided to break the curfew. He told his parents that he was just going to play footy with Frank and Ernest, the ankylosaur twins, and set off for No Man's Land.

The carnival was in full swing when he arrived. There was only a small gathering as most of the other herbivores had observed the curfew, but Darwin was glad about that. Normally it would be just his luck to be stuck behind a megasaurus in a wide-brimmed hat and struggle to see anything, but today there was no one to spoil his view.

The carnival queen was stunning, the costumes of mythical creatures sitting in the decorated floats were extremely convincing and, while the clowns were even less funny than usual, Darwin amused himself at the fun fair for hours.

Having been on the helter skelter, the bouncy castle and all the slot machines, he spent the last of his pocket money on a stick of candy floss and

a rickety trip round the House of Horrors. It
wasn't nearly as scary as the name suggested but
when he finally emerged, covered in artificial
cobwebs and looking to get his money back, he
was horrified to find that it was just as dark
outside as it had been inside with all the spooks
and skeletons. He'd been enjoying himself so
much, he hadn't noticed the time – his parents
would be going frantic.

The carnival had quite a different atmosphere in the evening. As the moon rose, it became far less friendly and a lot more menacing. Darwin had already spotted a gang of lesser carnivores behaving like buffoons near the rifle range and while he knew they were too small to kill him outright, they were very likely to mug him for the coconuts he'd won, nick his trainers and generally take the mick.

In order to avoid them, and because he needed to get home in a hurry, Darwin did the very thing his mother always told him not to do. Sidling past the burger stall, he took a shortcut through the deep, dank, dark Primeval Forest.

The last time Darwin had been in the forest, he'd been taking part in a marathon with his family and neighbours from Fossil Street. It had been during the Dinosaur Olympics, in which the Uptown herbivores attempted to bond with the Downtown carnivores – namely Flint Beastwood's blood-thirsty crew, including a particularly mean velociraptor called Liz Vicious, a thuggish deinosuchus with a head the size of a cello case named Mr Cretaceous, and a gibbering, dribbling pteranodon who answered to the name of Terry O'Dactyl.

Darwin shuddered as he remembered how Team Carnivore had tried to sabotage every single event. If he hadn't befriended Beastwood's slave Dippy Egg, the gentle gallimimus who warned him about Flint's foul play, he might not even be alive.

The forest was scary enough in the day and at night it was a very different kettle of coelacanth. Darwin was no coward, but the last time he felt this frightened was when he wandered into the meat market in Raptor Road and got lost looking for Uncle Loops.

As the moon slipped behind a cloud and the forest grew even darker, Darwin whistled to himself to keep his spirits up. As well as teaching him how to fart a tune, Uncle Loops had taught him to whistle and he was very grateful for the lesson because right now it was the only thing keeping him calm.

The strange rustling in the bushes was just the skittering of harmless, furry critters, he told himself. That hair-raising roar was merely the cry of a saber-toothed tiger calling her cubs. Those giant footprints he had just spotted in the mud simply belonged to a . . . Darwin took another look at them and froze.

Even in the dim light, he could see that the footprints were not only huge, they were the most peculiar shape – at least a metre long and oddly rounded at the toe. The distance between the strides was also alarmingly wide, which could mean only one thing: they belonged to an enormous species of dinosaur he had never seen before. Even worse, they were fresh.

Darwin cast his mind back to Boris's

description of the loathsome carnivore he'd seen in No Man's Land with its armoured scales and teeth like scythes, and he felt sick to his stomach. He wished he'd obeyed the curfew and stayed indoors and played Scrabble with Uncle Loops but, frightened as he was, part of him was curious and he couldn't resist following the monstrous tracks to see who had made them.

Holding his breath, he tiptoed gingerly along the trail, trying to calculate the size of the beast by the depth of its tread. He was surprised the footprints didn't show any signs of claws – after all, Uncle Loops claimed that whatever he saw had enormous ones. Then again, maybe it could sheath its claws like a saber-toothed tiger, and only whipped them out when it was hunting down a delicious little stegosaurus running through the forest all on its own.

A twig cracked behind him. Darwin almost

choked on his own whistle. He could hear an ominous *thump-thump*, *thump-thump* coming closer and closer. As he whipped round, fully expecting to stare death in the face, he saw a hideous form striding towards him through the shadows and he threw his head back and screamed, '*Australopithecus!*'

It was Ozzi up to his tricks again. He seemed a lot taller than usual too. This was because he was standing on a pair of circus stilts stolen from the carnival, but the trickery didn't stop there. Somehow he had also managed to wrestle a pair of gigantic clown shoes off its owner and secured them to the bottom of each stilt to make a pair of crazy feet. Not only that, he'd had the cheek to cut a couple of armholes in Uncle Loops's stolen cap and was using it as a duffel bag.

While it had taken thousands of years for his species to come down from the trees and walk about on two legs, amazingly it had only taken Ozzi the best part of an afternoon to perfect his stilt-walking. Armed with this new skill, he had deliberately and 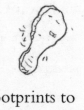 wickedly made a false trail of scary footprints to startle anyone stupid enough to be blundering round in the forest after sunset.

 'Why can't you use your ape-like intelligence to do something useful for society instead of picking on dinosaurs all the time?' yelled Darwin.

If the australopithecus had understood a single word, he didn't show it. He just bared his dirty teeth, snickered, and as Nogs, his mangy pet cynognathus, chewed on the clown shoes, he danced up and down on his stilts and taunted Darwin by wriggling his hairy bottom in his face.

'It's all a game to you, isn't it?' shouted Darwin. 'Don't think I've forgotten the time you swapped my swimming stuff for Uncle Loops's or the time you switched the signs at the swimming pool and made me dive into the shallow end.'

He was embarrassed that he'd been made a fool of yet again and although he was by nature a peace-loving herbivore, he was angry now. The sight of Ozzi sticking his tongue out and mocking him was more than he could bear.

'Right, that does it!' yelled Darwin, aiming a swift kick at the left stilt. Although he had stumpy legs, he was good shot and his foot connected with a satisfying, wood-splintering *craaaack*. Ozzi's bulging brow collapsed into an anxious frown as he began to wobble.

'That's for trying to scare me just now!' said Darwin, aiming another good kick at the right stilt. 'And *that's* for taking Uncle Loops's cap. How dare you pick on a pensioner!'

It was a killer blow. Suddenly, Ozzi lost his grip, teetered about haphazardly for a few seconds, then with a startled look on his face, he accidentally did the splits. As he tried in vain to control the left stilt, the right stilt shot up in the air, catapulting the clown shoe into a tree and dumping Ozzi head-first into a puddle.

'I'm sorry, but it's your own fault,' said Darwin.

Ozzi lay in a crumpled heap. Despite the fact

that Ozzi got on his nerves, Darwin was a kind soul and worried that he was seriously hurt.

He should have saved his pity. Ozzi sat up, rubbed his head and, with an evil glint in his eye, he reached into his make-shift duffel bag, pulled out a catapult and loaded it with a rock.

Darwin backed away slowly as the australopithecus aimed it between his eyes.

'Hey, I'm unarmed! Don't shoot!' said Darwin. Just as Ozzi was about to fire, Nogs let out a pitiful whimper, cowered with his tail between his

legs and covered his eyes with his paws. Reading
his unmistakable body language, Ozzi dropped his
catapault, then he too leapt up and down,

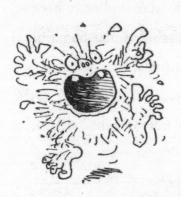 showing the whites of
his eyes, and pointed
wildly in the direction
of Darwin's back.
'Ha, ha, very funny,
Ozzi,' tutted Darwin.
'There's nothing behind
me. I'm not falling for that old trick.'

But this time, Ozzi wasn't joking. His little
bowed legs were shaking like jelly, his hair was
standing on end and, with a yelp, he turned and
scampered off in terror. Darwin turned round
slowly, his heart pounding, and saw why.

'Gotcha!' growled an all too familiar voice.

CHAPTER 3

BEASTWOOD IS BACK

Darwin's jaw dropped. Standing directly behind him was his worst nightmare come true. It wasn't the hideous, armour-plated, spikey-tailed new carnivore that he'd been expecting – it was four times more terrifying than that.

He was being eyeballed by a particularly

nasty-looking T. Rex, a scar-faced deinosuchus with thighs as thick as tree trunks, a foul-smelling, skittering pteranodon with a lazy eye and a sneering velociraptor in a skimpy dress. In other words, he was surrounded by Flint Beastwood's grisly gang from Raptor Road and, for some unknown reason, they didn't look very pleased with him.

'Shall I snap his head off now, Boss?' muttered the burly deinosuchus, flexing his biceps and clattering his fangs menacingly close to Darwin's snout.

Flint Beastwood considered it for a moment, then flicked his henchman playfully with a withered thumb and finger.

'Less haste, Mr Cretaceous. We must bide our time. There's no point in killing the little chap until we have some answers.'

The pteranodon seemed deeply disappointed. 'Can I not at least poke his eyes out with my beak, Boss?' tittered Terry O'Dactyl, flapping his skinny leather wings over-excitedly and hopping in mad circles.

The T. Rex shook his great head. 'Later, my psychotic little terror-saur.'

He sighed, turning to the raptor. 'Pass me that long, thick rope, please, Elizabeth.'

The velociraptor looked at Darwin sideways and mentally measured his throat. 'You're never gonna strangle him, Beastie, are you? It'll take forever. I know he's only a little veggie but he takes a large collar size by the looks of him.'

'Liz is right. You don't want to strangle the poor little fella,' argued Terry O'Dactyl. 'That'd be a terrible wicked thing and no mistake. You want to hang him, so you do. Shall I string him up by his dingle and dangle him right now, Boss?'

As they argued amongst themselves about whether to dangle him by his dingle or dingle him by his dangle, Darwin began to feel less afraid and more annoyed. It wasn't the first time he'd been cornered by carnivores but he was determined it would be the last.

'Excuse me!' he interrupted as they fought over the rope. 'Excuse me, but what exactly have I done to upset you, Mr Beastwood?'

Flint swivelled and fixed him with a black, beady eye. 'I think you know perfectly well.'

'No I don't,' insisted Darwin.

'Oh yes you do!' chorused the gang.

Darwin honestly didn't have a clue what they meant but no matter how hard he protested his innocence, Flint Beastwood didn't believe him.

'What are you doing all alone in the forest at this time of night?' he demanded. 'A little veggie like you should be tucked up fast asleep in bed unless he's up to no good.'

'I went to the carnival. It was so much fun, I didn't realise how late it was,' explained Darwin. 'If you want proof, I'll show you my coconuts.'

'He's got a lovely bunch of coconuts. See them all lined up in a row?' warbled Terry O'Dactyl, attacking the hairy shells with his beak, but Flint Beastwood wasn't convinced. He stroked the underside of Darwin's chin with his claw, breathing in his face. 'I think you're hiding something from me, Darwin.'

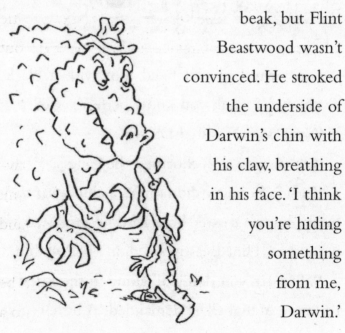

Darwin shrugged and looked completely bemused. 'Me? Hiding something? Like what?'

'Oh, very clever,' said Flint, clapping, 'but it's not a *what* – as well you know – it's a *who* and it isn't any old who you are hiding, is it?'

'What? How?' exclaimed Darwin. 'I haven't hidden a who.'

Flint Beastwood tutted impatiently and reached for the rope. 'Am I going to have to tie you up and let Mr Cretaceous beat the truth out of you?'

'Oh go on, let me,' said the deinosuchus. 'It'll make me feel so much better.'

As Mr Cretaceous put his massive, claw-studded fists up and blundered towards him, Darwin considered the offer for a moment and ducked out of the way.

'I'd rather you didn't. My parents will be furious. They've already lost their oldest son to a carnivore and, apart from that, beating me up won't do you any good because I'm not hiding anything. I swear on my Uncle Loops's life.'

Even the thickest carnivore among them knew how much Darwin loved his uncle.

Mr Cretaceous took his boss to one side and had a quiet word with him. 'You're wasting yer time, Boss. That little sprout don't know diddy squit about Dippy's whereabouts. Let's face it, he's done a runner. He's probably left the flaming forest by now.'

Being a deinosuchus, his quiet word was rather loud, and when Darwin heard Dippy's name mentioned, he was anxious to know what had happened to his good friend. He knew Dippy was desperately unhappy working for Flint and had been for a long time. He'd listened to the gentle gallimimus's tale of woe the night he'd been kidnapped by Beastwood.

Dippy had been meant to guard Darwin at the time, but taking pity on the little stegosaurus who was so far away from his home in Uptown, he had secretly untied him, brought him nice things to eat and told him his life story.

It was a very sad one, as Darwin recalled. Dippy Egg had been orphaned as a baby and was found wandering in the forest by Liz Vicious. She took him back to Flint's penthouse suite above his seedy club known as The Prehysterical.

Beastwood agreed to look after him, but he had no interest in Dippy's welfare whatsoever – he merely adopted him because he wanted a slave. Ever since, he'd bullied Dippy, insulted him and fed him things that would even make a deinosuchus puke. By the time Darwin met him, the poor gallimimus was almost starving.

Darwin hated cruelty of any kind and as it became clear that Dippy had finally managed to escape from Flint's clutches, he felt like dancing for joy. Dippy had great hopes of going to university and getting a degree in quantum physics and now maybe his dream would come true.

'I'm going to ask you one more time,' said Beastwood, pacing up and down. 'Darwin Stigson, have you any idea where that cracked, runny, Dippy Egg might have gone to? Is he round at your house?'

'No,' said Darwin firmly. 'I haven't seen Dippy since the Dinosaur Olympics when I beat him at the high jump.'

'Hmm,' said the T. Rex, tweaking Darwin's snout as if he was tuning in a radio. 'Only, rumour has is it that you two became friends behind my back.'

'Sweet,' said Liz Vicious.

Did Flint know for a fact that Darwin had taught Dippy to read or that Dippy had warned him about the cheating Team Carnivore had planned at the Olympics? Darwin didn't know for sure, but the last thing he wanted to do was drop Dippy in it.

'I liked Dippy,' admitted Darwin. 'He was gentle and kind but I have no idea where he has gone and now I'm really worried about him.'

'Why is that, my little radish?' sneered Flint. 'Are you worried because Mr Cretaceous is going to tear him limb from limb when we catch up with him?'

Mr Cretaceous's eyes lit up at the thought.

'No,' said Darwin.

'Ah!' said Flint. 'Then are you worried because Terry O'Dactyl is going to gore him to death and rip out his innards?'

'No,' said Darwin, cringing at the thought. 'I'm worried that Dippy has been eaten by the gigantic, vicious new carnivore that is wandering around these parts.'

Flint stopped looking smug and seemed somewhat alarmed. 'You're making it up,' he said.

'No, it's true, I swear,' said Darwin. 'It's been seen by several herbivores. It's a monstrous thing. That's why Boris the mayor has imposed a curfew. No one is supposed to go to No Man's Land. It's too dangerous.'

Flint Beastwood looked thoughtful. 'Is it bigger than me?'

'Much bigger,' said Darwin. 'It's bigger than all four of you put together and twice as mean. It's got armoured scales, a spikey tail, huge fangs and —'

It was all too much for Mr Cretaceous. By the way his knees were knocking, he seemed genuinely scared.

'I don't like the sound of this, Boss,' he muttered. 'If it's bigger than all of us, we should forget about Dipstick and clear off. There ain't much meat on a gallimimus, anyway. What if it's still hungry?'

Flint, having recovered from the initial shock, was more angry than scared. He was furious to think that his slave might have been eaten – not out of pity's sake, but because he'd have to find a replacement and that was a nuisance. Gallimimi made the best slaves because they were so eager to please, but orphans weren't that easy to come by. He'd have to kill some adult ones, which was tricky because the mothers had a particularly strong kick.

Even worse, he suspected that if this new carnivore was as big and fierce as it was cracked up to be, it was only a matter of time before it made its way to Raptor Road, broke into his headquarters at The Prehysterical, murdered him in his bed and took over his empire.

'I'm not having it!' he raged. 'I am going to hunt the beast down!'

'See ya,' said Mr Cretaceous.

'Good luck with that, Boss!' snickered Terry O'Dactyl. 'I'll be off now to visit me sick granny. What flowers will you be wanting at your funeral?'

Even Liz Vicious was having doubts and was sidling away in her stilettos.

'What, is this mutiny?' bellowed Flint.

'Elizabeth, where are you going?'

The velociraptor looked at him sheepishly. 'The nail bar?'

As Flint tried to rally his gang into action, Darwin seized the opportunity to escape and tiptoed away into the forest. He'd only gone a few steps when Beastwood swung round and spotted him creeping off.

'This is all your fault, you mouldy little grass muncher!' he yelled.

'No it isn't,' retorted Darwin, 'I'm just the messenger.'

For a moment, Flint Beastwood said nothing. Then, waving his tiny little arms in frustration, he barked this simple order to his ruthless gang: 'Kill the messenger!'

It was music to Mr Cretaceous's ears — dispatching a small stegosaurus was going to be so much easier and much more fun than

grappling with the great unknown.

'Will do, Boss. Let's get him, Terry!' he bellowed.

Darwin gulped. The foul foursome re-grouped and came thundering towards him. Darwin zig-zagged off through the trees as fast as he could but, as the velociraptor hurdled over the bushes towards him and the pteranodon breathed down his neck, he was beginning to wonder if his fastest was fast enough. Darwin was running for his life.

CHAPTER 4

ENTER THE DRAGON

Darwin might not have been able to outrun the Downtown Dinosaurs but, being smarter than the average stegosaurus, he reckoned he could outwit them. Noticing that the crescent moon was about to be blotted out for a few seconds by a large cloud, he led Flint's gang down an avenue of trees that ended in a dead end of thorny brambles.

Taking advantage of those few precious seconds of total darkness, Darwin dived head first into an enormous pile of fallen leaves until he was completely hidden from view, and held his breath. As the moon reappeared from behind the cloud, Flint realised with great annoyance that he'd lost his quarry and promptly laid the blame on his henchman.

'That slimy little stegosaur has given us the slip!' he snapped. 'Where were you, Mr Cretaceous? You're all talk! You go around giving it large, but actually you're as much use as a chocolate teapot!'

Mr Cretaceous swore under his fishy breath and immediately blamed O'Dactyl.

'I almost had him, Boss,' he said. 'I woulda done if that idiot Terry-saur hadn't flown across the face of the moon and blocked out all my light.'

Furious at this accusation, the pteranodon scuttled over and without a word of warning, he jabbed the deinosuchus in the left eyeball with his beak.

'That was not *me* flying in front of the moon, Mr C!' screeched Terry.

The deinosuchus clutched his eye and grabbing the skeletal pteranodon by the tail, began to whirl him around violently.

'Argh, no! Stop it now! I'm all dizzy, I'll be

sick, so I will!' wailed O'Dactyl.

'Watch out, you nearly had me over!' yelled Liz Vicious, staggering as she was whipped behind the knees by the pteranodon's spinning head. She kicked Mr Cretaceous up the backside in retaliation. Flint Beastwood felt it was his duty to pile in. As the carnivores tried to beat each other to a pulp, Darwin crawled out from beneath the heap of leaves and silently slipped away.

By now, he was cold, tired, and had completely lost his bearings. Rather than making his way towards the treeline as he'd hoped, he found that he'd wandered deeper into the Primeval Forest. Every hoot, crack and caw filled him with dread – whistling to himself no longer seemed to help and, even worse, a storm was brewing.

As the thunder crashed and the lightning flashed, Darwin ran blindly through sheets of rain, blundered through a thick curtain of creepers and found himself inside a cave.

Wringing out his sopping wet hat, he sat down on a rock, caught his breath and took in his surroundings. It was impossible to tell how deep the cave was because the far end was plunged in darkness but near the front it was illuminated by the watery sparks of stars that had managed to penetrate through the gaps in the cave roof.

It was surprisingly warm and dry inside and apart from a few small bats and beetles it looked like he had the place to himself. To the left of him, he was pleased to note there was a bed-sized stone shelf covered in thick moss jutting out from the wall. Exhausted, Darwin lay down on it and curled up. It wasn't as soft as his mattress at home and he could have done with a pillow, but he was so tired, he

fell asleep almost as soon as he'd shut his eyes.

In his sleep, he dreamt that Uncle Loops had stolen Flint Beastwood's moped from the car park behind The Prehysterical and had come to rescue him. However, as soon as he got to the forest, it had all gone horribly wrong because the australopithecus had secretly filled the petrol tank with custard powder, shaving foam and ball bearings.

The resulting series of explosions had caused Uncle Loops to lose control of the bike, which did a wheely and went into a dramatic skid.

There was an almighty crash and, still half-asleep, Darwin sat bolt upright and shouted, 'Uncle, is that you?'

Rubbing his eyes, he woke fully with a start. Blinking at the bright beams of early dawn light poking through the cave, he was suddenly, horribly aware that he wasn't alone. Something was shuffling about in the shadows right at the back of the cave and by the sounds of it, it wasn't Uncle Loops.

Darwin froze. He had a very creative imagination – what if this cave was the unknown, dreaded carnivore's lair? Had it been in there all night long, watching him while he slept and licking its lips?

In his mind's eye, he could see the shadowy form of the ferocious carnivore growing larger, hungrier and more terrible by the second. The deadly echo of its footsteps were getting nearer and nearer. There was no escape, it was too late for him to hide.

STOMP
STOMP
STOMP!

It was almost upon him. It was going to eat him. Darwin put his hands over his eyes and wished with all his heart that he'd listened to Boris and obeyed the curfew.

'Goodbye, Mum,' he whispered. 'Goodbye, Dad. Goodbye, dear old Uncle Loops.'

He braced himself and waited for the end to come.

'Blimey, it's you!' said a muffled voice. 'Are you all right, mate?'

Darwin opened his eyes and peered through his fingers. Standing in front of him was what appeared to be a massive carnivore with red eyes, a spikey tail and armoured scales. It fitted Sir Tempest's description perfectly, but despite this, it seemed quite friendly. In fact, it seemed to have recognised him.

Even in the dim light, Darwin felt that something didn't quite ring true about this creature and on closer inspection, he noticed it had a zip which ran all the way down its front. Close-up, its scales seemed somewhat rubbery and the claws looked rather plastic.

'It's only me!' said Dippy.

Darwin gave a huge sigh of relief as the gallimimus unzipped the padded dragon costume he was wearing and revealed his face.

'Sorry, didn't mean to scare you,' said Dippy, sitting down next to him. 'I nicked the suit from the carnival – good, innit?'

He encouraged Darwin to stroke the fabric.

'I hate stealing, I'm a good gallimimus, I am. But I have to be in disguise or Beastwood will hunt me down and capture me.'

His eyes brimmed with tears and he tilted his head backwards so they wouldn't fall. 'I don't want to be his slave no more,' he mumbled. 'I've run away.'

Darwin gave him a comforting pat on the back. 'I know. Mr Beastwood told me. I ran into him in the forest. He was out looking for you with his gang. He seemed to think I knew where you were for some reason.'

Dippy looked most concerned. 'You're

kidding, aren't cha? I never said nuthin to Beastwood about us. I'd never get you into trouble, Darwin, not with you being my only friend. He didn't hurt you, did he?'

Darwin shook his head. 'He was going to. He threatened to dangle me, strangle me and all sorts.'

'He did that to me an' all,' said Dippy mournfully. 'I've been strangled and dangled more times than I can remember. Got used to it in the end.'

He grabbed hold of his own skinny neck, bulged his eyes and lolled his tongue as if he'd just been hanged and though he tried to turn it into a joke, it was clear to Darwin that

Dippy had never really got used to the cruelty that Flint Beastwood had dished out daily. In fact, he'd developed several nervous tics, including a rather disturbing eye twitch.

'What made you leave in the end?' he asked.

The gallimimus shuddered and Darwin felt mean for asking.

'Sorry, you don't have to tell me if it's too painful.'

'No, no,' said Dippy, 'I need to get it off me chest. He wanted me to . . .'

He gagged at the memory and his twitchy eye went into overdrive.

'He wanted me to . . . to clean his *toenails!*'

Darwin felt his gorge rise. 'Eeeugh, that's gross! Did you actually go through with it?'

The gallimimus cringed and pulled a face. 'You should have seen what come out. Ooh, it was horrible. Anyhow, that was the last straw. I spiked his cocoa with laxatives and while he'd got the runs, I did a runner. Want some breakfast, mate?'

Despite all the talk of T. Rex's toenails, Darwin's stomach was rumbling and he suddenly realised he hadn't eaten a thing since lunchtime the day before.

'What is there to eat?'

'I could do you a nice wild mushroom omelette,' said Dippy, reaching into the back of the cave and producing a frying pan.

Darwin could see that Dippy had really made himself at home there. He'd built himself a little kitchen and gathered a variety of edible herbs, roots and berries from the forest which he'd put in jars or hung from the ceiling. There was also a large pot of Russian caviar with Beastwood's name on it.

'How long have you been living in this cave?' exclaimed Darwin.

'Dunno,' said Dippy. 'Ain't got a watch. I never learnt to tell the time, anyway.'

He broke some eggs into the pan and as he whisked them up with a stick, for once in his life he looked really happy and relaxed. Darwin thought it was a pity he couldn't live there forever, but it was too dangerous. Flint was bound to catch up with him sooner or later.

'What are your plans, Dippy?' he asked as they tucked into their mushroom omelettes.

Dippy shrugged. 'I'm going to California,' he mumbled with his mouth full. 'Don't know if you've ever heard of it? It's a little place near Scotland.'

As far as Darwin knew, California was nowhere near Scotland, unless the continents had shifted dramatically again.

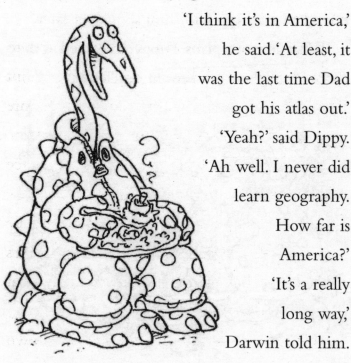

'I think it's in America,' he said. 'At least, it was the last time Dad got his atlas out.' 'Yeah?' said Dippy. 'Ah well. I never did learn geography. How far is America?' 'It's a really long way,' Darwin told him.

'You'd have to take a boat to get there. It's not impossible, but there is one big problem . . .'

'What's that?' asked Dippy.

'Getting out of this forest in one piece,' said Darwin.

'I'll be all right,' said Dippy. 'Beastwood will never recognise me in this dragon costume. It's proper realistic, ain't it?'

It took some while to explain that thanks to the description Darwin gave him, Flint Beastwood was now hunting down a creature that looked exactly the same as Dippy's costume in the mistaken belief that it was a fierce carnivore hell-bent on destroying him.

'I think he's even more keen to kill it than he is to capture you,' sighed Darwin. 'I'm sorry. It's all my fault, but if you wander about in that costume, you're as good as dead.'

The gallimimus slid the zip up and down

sadly and stared at his toes. 'Might as well give myself up, then,' he murmured. 'Once a slave, always a slave.'

He got up, shuffled off sadly with the eggy plates and began to wash them up. Darwin ran over to help him. He couldn't bear to think of his friend going back to his dreadful old life.

'Dippy, don't give up. There's no way you're going back to cleaning Flint's toenails,' he insisted.

'I'll think of a plan to help you escape, I promise.'

'Yeah?' Dippy beamed. 'Would you really do that for me? Nobody's ever done nice things for me. That would be great, because I have this dream of getting a degree.'

'In quantum physics.' Darwin nodded. 'I remember you telling me.'

The gallimimus put his head on one side and looked thoughtful. 'What is quantum physics, Darwin?' he said.

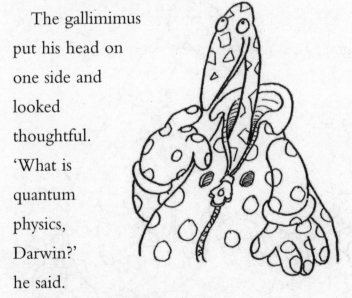

'I'm sure you'll find out when you start studying,' said Darwin breezily.

Whether Dippy got out of the forest alive, let alone went to university, was all down to Darwin. It was a huge responsibility and to Darwin's dismay, he couldn't think of a single plan.

But, for his friend's sake, he had to keep his promise somehow.

CHAPTER 5

A CUNNING PLAN

Meanwhile, back at Fossil Street, Darwin's parents were going frantic. He hadn't come home for his dinner the night before, which was most unusual. Being a growing stegosaurus, he had a very hearty appetite and, on top of that, he knew that his mother was cooking carrot frazzle – his favourite meal. He wouldn't have missed it for the world.

Dinner was usually at seven but by nine o'clock, Darwin still hadn't returned, the carrot frazzle had frizzled and it was far too dark for him to be playing football with the ankylosaur twins.

Mrs Stigson was getting concerned. 'I'm going to call Frank and Ernest's mother,' she announced.

'Lydia,' said Mr Stigson, 'you mollycoddle that boy. There's probably a perfectly reasonable explanation. He'll be round at their house playing ping pong or something.'

'He hates ping pong,' said Mrs Stigson. 'I'm going to ring up. If nothing else, it will put my mind to rest.'

But it didn't. When Frank and Ernest's mother answered the phone, she claimed that the twins had spent the afternoon at fencing classes and hadn't seen Darwin for days.

'Maurice, our son lied to us!' wailed Mrs Stigson. 'Why would he do that?'

'So he could have some fun,' said Uncle Loops. 'I bet he went to the carnival. That's what I'd do if I was one hundred and eighty years younger. He's been looking forward to it for weeks.'

'But there's a curfew!' said Mrs Stigson. 'None of us are allowed to go to No Man's Land in case we bump into that loathsome new carnivore. The mayor said so.'

'Curfew smurfew,' groaned Uncle Loops. 'Norris the mayor knows diddly squit. Rules are made to be broken. Want me to go and fetch young Damian?'

'I'll go,' said Mr Stigson, irritably. 'Knowing you, you'll get your backside stuck in the kiddies' roundabout like you did last year,

Augustus. And just for the record, the mayor is called Boris and your nephew's name is Darwin.'

'I know that, Malcolm,' snapped Uncle Loops. 'I never forget a name.'

Mr Stigson grabbed his coat and left.

'Be careful, Maurice,' called Mrs Stigson. 'It gets a bit rough up there after dark.'

Never had truer words been spoken. Lots of teenage carnivores hung around at the funfair in the evening, dominating the dodgem cars and causing trouble. On top of that, No Man's Land was australopithecus territory, which was always a worry.

Ozzi was a devil with a spanner and when the fairground rides came to town, he just couldn't resist undoing the nuts and bolts. As a result, by the time Mr Stigson arrived, the Big Wheel was rolling down the hill towards him full of screaming passengers and nearly ran him over.

He managed to leap out of the way just in time, only to find the fairground in full swing – apart from the swing boats which had swung completely upside down and got stuck horizontally in the air, dumping the unfortunate swingers onto the grass below. Mr Stigson was relieved to note that his son wasn't among the

casualties, who were receiving fist aid, rather than first aid, from a baryonyx wearing a blood-stained butcher's apron.

Maybe Darwin was in the arcade, playing the slot machines. Mr Stigson went to investigate but there was no sign of him and no one claimed to have seen him. Fortunately, the protoceratops manning the coconut shy was able to shed some light on the matter.

'Roll up, roll up, sir! Yes, I did see a little steggie answering to your lad's description. He won three coconuts. Maybe you could do even better, sir. Come along now, only a pound a throw, three balls for two pounds. You know you want to, sir.'

Mr Stigson didn't want to at all but the protoceratops was very pushy, so he reluctantly parted with his money and tried his luck while he interrogated the stall holder.

'How long ago did you see my boy?' he asked.

The protoceratops scratched his massive muzzle. 'Hours ago . . . Ohhh, you nearly had it right off its post, sir. Bad luck! Go on, sir, have three more balls, only a pound for you.'

'How many hours?' asked Mr Stigson, pelting the balls in frustration. 'One? Two?'

The protoceratops shrugged. 'Possibly three, sir. I sincerely hope young fellow-me-lad hasn't been foolish enough to take a shortcut through the Primeval Forest,' he added gravely. 'It's not safe at the best of times but with that new loathsome carnivore lurking around too? Oh dear, oh dear.'

'My son knows not to go in there at night. He'd never do a silly thing like that,' insisted Mr Stigson.

'Your nuts, sir,' said the protoceratops.

'I beg your pardon?' said Mr Stigson.

'Your coconuts. You knocked two down, sir.' The protoceratops handed them over and wished him all the best with finding Darwin.

'Oh, I expect he's safely indoors by now,' replied Mr Stigson airily. But he wasn't. His mother had been all round the houses, but no one had seen him since the afternoon. The Stigsons sat up all night with Uncle Loops waiting for Darwin to come home but by dawn the following day, he still hadn't returned and they were sick with worry.

Around the time the Stigsons normally had their elevenses, Mrs Merrick came round to give them her support, in exchange for several sticky buns and a bucket of cocoa. She was shortly followed by Sir Stratford Tempest who had nothing better to do now that the theatre was closed and Frank and Ernest, the ankylosaur twins, who had lots of better things to do but whose mother wanted them out from under her feet.

'At least she knows her sons are alive!' wailed Mrs Stigson. 'I lost my first-born to a tyrannosaurus and for all I know Darwin has already been eaten too.'

'I wish I'd already eaten,' said Mrs Merrick, slapping Mrs Stigson with her trunk to calm her down. 'Lydia, you're hysterical. There will be a perfectly reasonable explanation.'

'Yes, he's probably been torn limb from limb,' boomed Sir Tempest.

'You're not helping, Stratford,' said Mr Stigson as his wife began to sob. 'What we need is a strategy. Has anyone got a good idea?'

'I've got no idea, let alone a good one,' said Uncle Loops. 'Let's ask Doris.'

The herbivores looked at him quizzically.

'Doris who?' asked Mrs Merrick.

'Doris the Bear,' said Uncle Loops, waving through the window as Boris the mayor pedalled up to the Stigsons' front door on his trusty bicycle.

'I was just checking to make sure you all obeyed my curfew last night,' he announced. 'It is very important that you do so. It is more dangerous in No Man's Land than ever now. I've just come back from Raptor Road and according to the gossip at the meat market,

Beastwood and his gang are in the Primeval Forest trying to hunt the beast down.'

Mrs Stigson let out a gasp and clutched at her heart. 'But Darwin's out there!' she cried. 'If the terrible new carnivore doesn't get him, Beastwood will! What are his chances of coming back alive?'

'Absolutely nil, darling,' said Sir Tempest, swooning dramatically on the sofa.

'You're still not helping!' hissed Mr Stigson. 'Boris, you're the mayor. Think of something!'

'I already have,' said Boris. 'I'm extending the curfew. You are not allowed to go to No Man's Land in the day now either.'

Mrs Merrick snorted into her cocoa. 'As usual, there's a gaping flaw in your plan,' she harrumphed. 'I knew edmontonia were thick, but you take the biscuit.'

'He can't, you've eaten them all,' sighed Uncle Loops upturning the empty tin.

Boris looked offended. 'I'm sorry you don't approve of my plan, Mrs Merrick,' he said huffily, 'but it is my duty to keep the citizens of Fossil Street safe.'

'But my son is in peril!' cried Mrs Stigson. 'How are we going to rescue him if you won't let us go after him?'

Sir Tempest Stratford peered at her from behind a cushion. 'We?' he said. 'I can't go, my agent wouldn't hear of it. She needs me in one piece to play the lead in *The Lizard Of Oz*.'

Mrs Merrick snatched the cushion with her trunk and smacked him with it.

'Don't be such a coward, Stratford,' she said. 'Boris, lift your curfew immediately! We're *all* going to help the Stigsons rescue Darwin or my name isn't Phyllis Merrick!'

'All for one and one for all!' chorused Frank and Ernest, wearing Mrs Stigson's saucepans as helmets and duelling with their umbrellas.

Touched as he was by everyone's enthusiasm, Mr Stigson didn't want to be too hasty. 'We can't just go into the forest mob-handed,' he said. 'We're not just facing our old enemy. We have no idea what this new dinosaur is capable of.'

'Well, it's highly unlikely we'll be able to beat it in a game of fisticuffs,' huffed Sir Tempest. 'I've seen it, remember. Ooh, the muscles on it. It could have snapped me in half like a cracker.'

'Not helping,' said Mr Stigson wearily as Mrs Stigson stuffed her fist into her mouth to stop herself screaming.

'We need to outwit it,' said Boris. 'It shouldn't be too hard. We herbivores may have a reputation for being a bit slow, but that's nonsense.'

'Nonsense?' said Uncle Loops. 'If you think I'm fast, you're slower than I thought.'

While the rest of the room struggled to get their heads around that, Boris quickly got something out of the bottom of the fridge.

'To prove it, I have come up with a cunning plan,' he said, waving a cucumber in the air.

'We will enter the Primeval Forest disguised as vegetables!'

The room fell silent.

'It's foolproof,' persisted Boris. 'Carnivores never eat their greens. They're a bunch of salad dodgers. Come on, guys, work with me on this.'

Mrs Stigson had heard enough and grabbed her hat. 'I'm going to see Lou Gooby,' she said. 'If any one knows what to do, she will.'

Boris put his hands on his hips and scoffed. 'That old hippy? I don't think so. Just because she's big doesn't mean she's clever.'

Even so, the rest of the neighbours thought it was worth a try and with Boris tagging along grumpily, they went and found the old mamenchisaurus. She was busy contemplating why she didn't have a navel when they arrived.

'We've lost Darwin,' said Mrs Stigson and told her the whole story.

Lou Gooby listened patiently, then she closed her eyes.

'See? The poor old thing's lost the plot and gone to sleep,' muttered Boris.

'She's *thinking*,' said Mrs Merrick. 'You should try it sometime.'

A few minutes later, the mighty mamenchisaurus opened her eyes and spoke. 'Unknown carnivore may be most dangerous,' she said in her mysterious accent.

'You don't say?' said Boris sarcastically. 'I could have told you that ten minutes ago without all the joss sticks and meditation malarkey.'

Lou Gooby gazed at him hard until he shrivelled, then spoke her words of wisdom. 'Herbivores of Fossil Street, you must go to Primeval Forest in disguise.'

By now, Boris was beside himself. 'That was my idea!' he said. 'Didn't I say let's go in disguise as vegetables? Back me up here, Stratford. You remember me getting the cucumber out, surely.'

Lou Gooby waited for him to stop blathering and continued her train of thought. 'You will go to forest disguised as trees.'

The more they thought about it, the more the herbivores agreed it was a brilliant idea. To fool their enemies into thinking they were enormous cabbages or carrots was impossible – even Mr

Cretaceous wouldn't fall for that. But disguised as trees, there would be no problem with size. Heavily camouflaged with leaves and branches, they could creep right up to the carnivores and grab Darwin from right under their noses.

'I'll fetch my secateurs,' said Mr Stigson, brightly. 'Quickly, everyone. Let's go and gather foliage and branches . . . No, Uncle Loops, you may *not* use the chainsaw.'

There wasn't a moment to lose.

CHAPTER 6

BEASTWOOD GETS STUFFED

While the Stigsons and their neighbours busied themselves making tree disguises, unbeknown to them, Darwin was still sitting in a cave in the middle of the Primeval Forest. He'd been racking his brains for ages but still hadn't got a clue how he was going to get Dippy Egg to safety.

'Maybe Flint and his gang have got bored of hunting the unknown carnivore and gone home,' said Dippy. 'They're never going to find something that don't even exist.'

'But they don't *know* it doesn't exist because I told them it did!' groaned Darwin. 'I told them it looked just like your dragon costume ... Hang on, that's it!' he cried. 'The costume! Why didn't I think of it before?'

'Think of what?' asked Dippy.

Darwin clapped his hands together enthusiastically and explained. 'We can use the dragon costume as a lure,' he said. 'We will fool Flint Beastwood into thinking it's the real thing and while he's attacking it, we can escape.'

Dippy scratched his head. 'You've lost me there, mate. Can you run it past me a bit more slowly?'

'Take the costume off, Dippy,' said Darwin.

Dippy blushed. 'But I'm butt-naked underneath.'

'Oh please, I've seen it all before,' said Darwin dismissively. 'It's not like I've got any pants on, is it? You can borrow my hat if it makes you feel better.'

The shy gallimimus undid the zip, stepped out of the costume and handed it to Darwin.

'It's a bit sweaty,' he apologised. 'I haven't had a chance to wash.'

'That's fine, it'll make it smell more like a real beast,' said Darwin.

As it was, the costume didn't look anything like a fierce carnivore. Once he'd slipped it off, Dippy couldn't imagine how it was going to fool anyone, let alone a wily T. Rex like Flint. He held it up and gave it a shake to get the creases out.

'I don't mean to criticise but it looks a bit . . . flat,' commented Dippy.

'We're going to stuff it,' Darwin told him triumphantly. 'If we make a simple skeleton out of big sticks, we can put it inside the costume to make arms and legs, then all we have to do is pad the body out with grass and leaves and bingo!'

'Bingo?' mused Dippy. 'Does that make good stuffing?'

Darwin shook his head. 'Bingo is just a turn of phrase. It means the same as "Ta Da!" You'll learn all that when you go to university, I expect.'

Dippy smiled to himself dreamily. The prospect of getting a decent education would do wonders for his self-confidence. For too long, Flint Beastwood had made him think he was a dumb  bird-brain. His name didn't help matters. Maybe if he got his degree he'd change it to Egg Head.

'So we just stuff the costume with leaves and grass?'

Darwin nodded and, making sure there were

no carnivores lurking nearby, the two of them nipped out of the cave and gathered everything they needed.

By mid-morning, even Mr Cretaceous was becoming a little bored of hunting. He was suffering from a sore snout – Liz Vicious had bitten it during the night's brawl. The wound was throbbing and it was putting him in an even worse temper than usual.

'I'm going to kill someone in a minute!' he roared.

'I'm glad to hear it, that's why I employ you,' said Flint Beastwood. 'Just make sure the someone you kill is the carnivore who is plotting to overthrow me.'

Mr Cretaceous folded his arms defiantly. 'I don't reckon it's here, Boss,' he said. 'We've been walking round and round in flaming circles for hours.'

'Maybe he's gone to Raptor Road already,' tittered Terry O'Dactyl. 'Maybe he's at The Prehysterical and he's swivelling in your swivel chair and smoking your cigars, so he is!'

Beastwood slapped him on the beak and the mad pteranodon screeched, hopped about and wrapped its bony head inside its skinny wings.

'Silence!' roared Flint.

'Here, Beastie . . . I say . . . ' said the velociraptor, pointing into the distance.

'I've just asked for silence, Elizabeth,' he muttered. 'Just because you're not one of the lads, you still have to do as I s—'

He stopped mid-word and his beady black eyes began to glitter. 'There he is!' he whispered. 'There's that no good, mysterious carnivore . . . Do you see him leaning casually against that tree like he owns the place, Mr Cretaceous?'

The deinosuchus narrowed his eyes. 'Let's have a squint . . . Ohhhh yes. He's big but not as big as all four of us . . . '

He started to paw the ground and drool and Flint Beastwood struggled to hold him back.

'Patience, Mr C. This is a delicate situation. You can't just go charging in.'

Mr Cretaceous looked at him quizzically. 'Why not?'

'Because we're *all* going to charge in! On the count of three – one, two, three . . . *Chaaarrrrge!*'

As the gruesome foursome bounded towards their target with curdling screams and yells, Darwin and Dippy watched from their hiding place in the bushes. They could hardly contain their giggles as Flint and his gang attacked the stuffed dragon costume and tore it to shreds. In

their frenzy, it took the carnivores from Raptor Road some time before they realised their mistake, but by then Darwin and Dippy had sneaked back out through the forest and were safely home in Fossil Street.

It was Uncle Loops who let them in. He'd very much wanted to go with his family and neighbours to search for his nephew and had gone to a great effort to disguise himself as a gooseberry bush. However, Mr Stigson was worried that he'd slow everyone down and convinced him that someone needed to stay at home in case Darwin miraculously returned.

'It's a miracle!' cried Uncle Loops. 'You've bought a bird home.'

'You remember, Dippy,' said Darwin. 'He competed with me in the high jump at the Dinosaur Olympics . . . Why are you covered in twigs, Uncle Loops?'

Uncle Loops toyed with his gooseberries and tried to remember. 'Maybe I fell in the compost heap again? No, that's not it. It's all coming back to  me now. Fat Phyllis got hold of me and rolled me in glue and leaves.'

Dippy looked genuinely shocked. 'Darwin, why would anyone do that to your poor uncle? What kind of a dreadful creature is she?'

'A mastodon,' said Darwin, who was as confused as to why Mrs Merrick would stick foliage all over his aged relative, but as Loops hadn't offered an explanation, he didn't like to pry. It was then that he realised his parents were nowhere to be seen.

'Where are Mum and Dad?' he asked.

'Out looking for you,' said Uncle Loops. 'They've gone to rescue you from a terrifying carnivore. I told them you'd be fine but no one believed me.'

'That carnivore was only me in a costume,' added Dippy.

'Oh no it wasn't,' said Uncle Loops.

'Really it was,' said Darwin.

But Uncle Loops refused to back down. 'No,

it wasn't! Just because I'm one hundred and eighty, it doesn't mean I don't know what I'm talking about.'

'You're one hundred and ninety,' Darwin reminded him.

'Suddenly I've aged ten years? Well, that just about puts the tin hat on it,' he sulked. 'Talking of which, have you seen my cap?'

'Never mind your cap right now,' said Darwin, deciding not to mention just what Ozzi had done to it. 'Mum and Dad are in mortal danger. Forget the unknown carnivore, it doesn't exist.'

'Yes it does!' said Uncle Loops.

'No it doesn't,' continued Darwin, 'but Flint and his gang are out there. We've just played a trick on them – humiliated them! The Downtown Dinosaurs are going to be in serious killing mode if they get so much as a whiff of an Uptown herbivore now.'

He had dreadful visions of becoming an orphan like Dippy. Like all parents, his could be extremely annoying on occasions, but he'd never wish them to be eaten.

'It's all right, the neighbours have gone with them,' Uncle Loops reassured him. 'Flat Phillip, Sir Fatford Temptress, the anklesore twins and Horace the mayor.'

'They don't stand a chance,' said Darwin, panicking. 'Maybe if I run I'll be able to catch up with them before Flint finds them.'

'They'll be very hard to spot,' said Uncle

Loops, pointing in the direction of the garden shrubbery. 'They're disguised as trees. They were so convincing, I kissed that bush goodbye thinking it was your mother.'

'Even so, I'm sure I can recognise my own mother,' said Darwin. 'You stay here and make yourself at home, Dippy. I'm going after them. Wish me luck.'

Dippy grabbed him by the shoulder. 'I'll come with you. You're my friend. I've never had a friend before. I can't lose you now.'

But Darwin wouldn't hear of it, much as he

would have enjoyed the company. 'No, think of your degree. You can't put yourself back in danger. It's only a matter of time before Flint finds you. You need to get to the docks tonight and sail to America.'

'But you can't go into the Primeval Forest on your own,' protested Dippy.

'He doesn't have to.' Uncle Loops smiled. 'He can go with that new dinosaur I told you about.'

'There is *no* new dinosaur!' wailed Darwin.

'Yes there is,' said Loops. 'He's in my bed, having a lie-down.'

Darwin frowned. Uncle Loops may have been many things, but he wasn't a liar. He did sometimes confuse fantasy with reality, though, so to get rid of any doubt, he sat on Uncle Loops lap and they took the stairlift up to the bedroom, with Dippy following behind them.

'What the fli—' gasped Darwin.

There, in the bed, was a snake-necked, long-beaked dinosaur curled up asleep with its massive claws resting on top of the duvet cover.

From what Darwin could see, it had all the characteristics of a typical carnivore but Uncle Loops didn't seem the slightest bit afraid.

'Shhh, don't wake him,' whispered Loops. 'It's only a young therizinosaurus – the same one I saw in the forest. He was exhausted when I found him in the back garden.'

'What was he doing in the back garden?' squeaked Darwin.

'Hiding, but after your dad chopped all the branches off the tree, it wasn't so easy.'

The therizinosaurus began to stir. It flared its enormous nostrils and yawned, exposing rows of massive teeth. Then it opened its eyes and fixed them with a hard stare.

Darwin pressed himself against the wall and prepared to die.

CHAPTER 7

OZZI STRIKES AGAIN

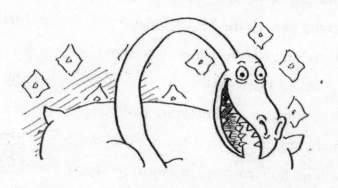

As the search party from Fossil Street headed towards No Man's Land disguised as trees, little did they realise that it was a completely pointless exercise. At that moment, Darwin was at home, wondering whether he was going to be eaten by a therizinosaurus, but they didn't know that as they marched into the Primeval Forest.

Mr Stigson insisted on following a particular route but ever since the Dinosaur Olympics, when Ozzi had switched the signposts and tricked him into leading Team Herbivore straight into a swamp, nobody trusted his navigation skills. Much to his annoyance, Mrs Merrick had put herself in charge.

'Boris suggested I put myself forward,' she insisted.

'Is that so?' said Mr Stigson unhappily. 'There must be some mistake. My observational skills are legendary. Excuse me while I have words with Boris.'

He stormed off to the back of the line of fake trees. 'Now look here, Boris. You might be the mayor but with all due respect, I'm beginning to question your sanity. I wouldn't leave Phyllis Merrick in charge of a swiss roll let alone a search party.'

Mr Stigson waited patiently for a reply and when Boris failed to answer, it had to be Mrs Merrick who explained why.

'You're talking to a rhododendron bush, Maurice!' she explained. 'I admit it looks a bit like Boris but he's not here, dear. He had to fulfil his duties at the town hall.'

Cringing with embarrassment, Mr Stigson stepped back into line next to his wife.

'You might have told me, Lydia,' he grumbled.

'It was an easy mistake to make,' she lied.

Mr Stigson wasn't the only one to get it in the neck from the overly bossy mastodon. She'd had it in for Sir Tempest ever since he ate the last custard cream.

'For heaven's sake, stand up straight, Stratford!' she trumpeted. 'You look as if you've got dutch elm disease.'

The triceratops waved his branches at her and looked deeply offended. 'Phyllis Merrick, how dare you? I'm not an elm, I am a weeping cherry!' he declared. 'You seem to forget that I had a very large part in a film called *The Tree Musketeers*. My agent said it was the most wooden performance she'd ever seen.'

'That's not the best of reviews, is it?' snorted the mastodon.

'It is if you're a mighty oak,' he retorted, 'but

if you think for one minute you look like a silver birch, you are sadly mistaken, madam; their trunks are a lot more slender.'

Mrs Stigson sighed. Along with the prickly foliage strapped to her body, the neighbours were beginning to rub her up the wrong way. Her husband was sulking, Sir Tempest and Mrs

Merrick were arguing non-stop and the ankylosaur twins seemed to think they were on a jolly day out – she was constantly having to remind them that bushes don't run around and to keep the noise down.

'Frank and Ernest, we're supposed to be creeping up on the carnivores in order to get my only son back. If you keep whooping, you're going to give our position away.'

The twins looked properly ashamed. 'Sorry, Mrs Stigson. I didn't mean go "Yeeeee-ha!"' shouted Ernest, frankly.

'And I didn't mean to go "Ya-hoo!"' yelled Frank, earnestly.

There was a strange rustle in the bushes.

'Was that you, Phyllis?' boomed Sir Tempest.

'No!' she hissed. 'Get your hands off my undergrowth! There's someone out there – they've heard us! Quick, act like a forest!'

The herbivores fell silent, assumed their best tree poses – hardly easy when they were expecting to come face to face with their arch enemies, the Downtown Dinosaurs.

'It might not be them. It might be that hideous, mysterious carnivore I told you about,' whispered Sir Tempest loudly.

'Stop quivering, Stratford,' replied Mrs Merrick. 'You'll lose your cherries!'

They heard a snuffling sound and, to their extreme annoyance, a cynognathus bounded into the clearing, frothing at the mouth and yapping. It was Nogs and, excited by so many tree trunks gathered in a row, he ran over and cocked his leg.

'My ankles have gone suddenly warm,' squeaked Sir Tempest.

'Don't be a fusspot. It'll wash off. Now shush!' muttered Mrs Merrick. 'Mark my words, if Nogs is here, that little beggar Ozzi can't be far behind.'

As if on cue, the australopithecus burst into the clearing. The herbivores struggled to keep quiet and not scold him for all the tricks he played on them – the carnivores from Raptor Road could turn up at any time, and so could the Even Scarier Unknown Carnivore.

'See that bag full of firewood he's wearing on his back?' whispered Mr Stigson. 'Does it look familiar to you, Lydia?'

'Good grief!' said Mrs Stigson. 'It's Uncle Loops's cap. It looks beyond mending.' Oblivious to the fact that he was surrounded by dinosaurs, Ozzi got down on his hairy knees and began to build a fire out of the twigs he'd collected in his duffel bag.

After a short while, it became quite clear to his sub-human brain that he didn't have enough wood. He whipped out a flint axe and began to advance on the cherry tree that stood before him. Swinging the axe around his head, he took aim at its trunk.

'Naff off!' screamed Sir Tempest, lashing out at the australopithecus in a very un-tree-like fashion. 'Run like the wind! He's got his chopper out!'

As the fake forest scattered left and right in fear of losing their limbs, Ozzi's great, furry eyebrows almost shot over the back of his head. His species had originally lived in trees and he

thought he'd got the measure of them, but these ones were behaving very strangely. Having got over the initial shock, his hunting instincts kicked in and, just as a dog can't resist chasing a ball, he ran after the escaping trees brandishing his weapon.

If Ozzi hadn't tripped over Nogs and twisted his ankle, any one of the Uptown herbivores might have ended up on the bonfire. But with Ozzi injured, they were able to give him the slip and came to rest in a glade a short distance away.

'I've had just about enough of this!' moaned Sir Tempest. 'As an actor, I'm happier than the next person to dress up, but this is beyond the call of duty. I'm sure I've got splinters.'

'Never mind your splinters, did any one think to bring a picnic?' said Mrs Merrick.

When no one offered any food, and when she thought no one was looking, Mrs Merrick started to pick at the fruit hanging in tempting bunches from Sir Tempest's branches.

'Don't you pinch my cherries!' he snapped. 'You'll ruin my disguise.'

Mrs Stigson adjusted a piece of holly that was digging into a very awkward place and tried to rally the troops who were clearly on the point of giving up and going home.

'We can't leave yet!' she said. 'Think of poor Darwin. He's out here all alone.'

Suddenly, she heard heavy footsteps crashing through the bracken and the sound of a horribly familiar voice. Her blood ran cold.

'I swear that tricky, sticky, little stegosaurus is here somewhere,' it said. 'I wouldn't want to be him when we find him.'

As Flint Beastwood and his gang strode into the glade, the Uptown herbivores hastily assumed their positions as trees again and froze.

Exhausted and running on empty after escaping from Ozzi, Mrs Merrick had been having a little lie-down, and when the Downtown Dinosaurs arrived unannounced she hadn't had time to stand up again. She was heavily disguised with layers of bark and so the somewhat short-sighted deinosuchus mistook her for a pile of logs and sat on top of her.

'I cannot believe you fell for Darwin Stigson's ridiculous stuffed dragon costume, Mr Cretaceous!' roared Flint. 'What kind of an idiot are you?'

'He's an even bigger eejut than me!' tittered Terry O'Dactyl, perching in Sir Tempest's lofty boughs. 'Fancy tinkin it was an ferocious mystery carnivore, Mr C. I'd never mistake a pretend dinosaur for a real one, so I wouldn't.'

Sir Tempest tried his best not to sneeze as the potty pteranodon's tail tickled his top lip.

'Why is everybody picking on me?' demanded the deinosuchus. 'It's Liz who's to blame, Boss. She was the one who pointed to it.'

Liz pulled a face and aimed a rock at his skull.

'Elizabeth, if you're going to throw heavy

objects at Mr Cretaceous, at least aim for a vital organ,' yelled Beastwood. 'Hitting him on the head won't achieve anything.'

Flint was never in the best of moods but the herbivores had never seen him this angry before.

'What are we going to do now, Beastie?' whined Liz Vicious. 'We've searched this forest high and low and there's still no sign of the little veggie. Maybe he's gone back to his mummy and daddy.'

Flint Beastwood screwed up his tiny eyes into pinholes. 'And maybe he's taken that long streak of a gallimimus with him,' he growled. 'I tell you what we're going to do. We are going to go to Fossil Street and pay the Stigsons a little visit and when we get there . . .'

The deinsosuchus leapt up and smashed his fist into his own palm excitedly. 'Can I break their door down, Boss?'

'Yes, Mr Cretaceous, indeed you may,' said Beastwood. 'You have my permission to break down their door, wreck their furniture, rip the doors off their cupboards and —'

'Smash their toilet seat?' begged Mr Cretaceous, who was by now dribbling uncontrollably at the thought of the havoc he was going to cause.

Flint Beastwood nodded and his face split into a ghastly smile. 'And once you have discovered Dippy Egg's hiding place, you and Mr O'Dactyl will drag him back by his boney beak to The Prehysterical where he will continue to be my slave. As for little Darwin, what shall we do with him? He has angered me greatly . . .'

Flint paused dramatically and stroked his chin as the gang came up with suitable suggestions.

'Nurdle him in the doobries, Boss!' offered Mr Cretaceous.

'Push him through the mincer!' screeched Terry O'Dactyl. 'Rub him with a cheese grater! Fry him in lard!'

Flint Beastwood shook his head. 'You're not trying hard enough, lads,' roared the tyrannosaurus. 'Nurdling, mincing and such like will seem almost enjoyable compared to what I have in mind. Nobody but nobody makes a fool out of me and gets away with it!'

With that, he punched the air with his tiny arm and stomped off out of the Primeval Forest towards the Stigsons' house with his motley crew in tow. As soon as they were out of sight, Mr Stigson did his best to comfort his wife.

'Look on the bright side, Lydia,' he said. 'At least we know Darwin is still alive.'

'Yes, but for how long?' she cried. 'If he's not in the forest, perhaps he *has* gone home ... How are we going to help him now?'

'Do something, Phyllis!' said Maurice. 'You're

supposed to be in charge.' But for once, even Mrs Merrick was completely stumped.

CHAPTER 8

THE ORPHAN OMNIVORE

'Right!' said Mr Stigson. 'You can take a back seat from now on, Phyllis. I'm taking over.'

Mrs Merrick gave him a very cold look. 'I'd like to see you do better, Maurice,' she grunted, trying to turn herself upright. 'I was going to step down anyway. I can't possibly carry on; all four of my limbs are completely paralysed.'

'Perhaps it's the stress,' said Mrs Stigson.

'No it isn't,' insisted Mrs Merrick, 'it's being sat upon by a hefty, great deinosuchus. I have a crushed spine. I may never walk again.'

Sir Tempest produced a chocolate muffin from somewhere about his person and waved it temptingly in the air near the mastodon's trunk. As she went to grab it, he whisked it out of reach – whereupon she sprang to her feet, wrestled it off him and tossed it down her throat without stopping to chew.

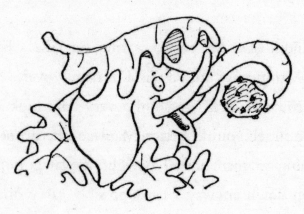

She sighed deeply as the muffin hit the spot. 'I'm much better now, Maurice,' she said. 'You can go back to being my second in command, dear.'

'Just because you're cured, you needn't think you can take over again, Phyllis,' said Mr Stigson huffily. 'Darwin is my son. I'm personally responsible for his safety. Beastwood's gang think he's run home – we have to beat them back to Fossil Street before they beat him up. In order to do this, we'll take the shortcut through those bushes, run as fast as we can —'

'I'm not running,' said Mrs Merrick, passing wind like a thunderclap. 'It's undignified.'

Mr Stigson refused to be put off. 'We will run ahead of the Downtown Dinosaurs,' he continued, 'and, standing closely together in our tree disguises, we will form a maze from which they cannot escape.'

'A *maze?*' spluttered Mrs Merrick. 'There are only six of us. Flint Beastwood will find his way out in seconds.'

'Not if we keep shifting about,' said Mr Stigson, adding to his plan as he went along. 'If we keep blocking their path, eventually they will get tired and fall asleep.'

'Really?' said Mrs Merrick sarcastically. 'Maybe you'd like me to sing them a lullaby while we're at it, to speed things up?'

'Don't be ridiculous, Phyllis,' said Sir Tempest, 'you can't sing for toffee, but I can for a small fee.'

Mrs Stigson could see that her husband was starting to crumble under all the criticism, so she decided to intervene.

'I think it's a great idea, Maurice,' she said. 'The carnivores are bound to give up and go to sleep eventually. When they do, we can run

home and barricade the house to keep Beastwood and his gang out.'

'My thinking exactly, Lydia,' said Mr Stigson, who'd thought nothing of the sort.

It was not the greatest plan in the world, but as nobody had a better one, the grumbling group of Uptown herbivores had little choice but to give it a go.

They freshened up their disguises and took the shortcut off the beaten track, moving as swiftly as they could under the weight of all the

leaves, branches and twigs, and attempted to get
ahead of the carnivores and corner them.

Just as Darwin's parents were preparing to rescue
him, *he* was figuring out how to rescue *them*.
Although he was still reeling from the shock of
finding a fierce-looking, random dinosaur
having forty winks in Uncle Loops's bed, he was
even more surprised when the dinosaur sat up,

took one
look at him
and burst
into tears.

'Never
judge a book
by its cover,
Darwin,' said
Uncle Loops

as he handed the tearful creature his grubby

handkerchief. 'I told you he was friendly.'

The therizinosaurus drew his huge, feathery knees up under his chin and blew his beak loudly, but he had such long claws, he dropped the hanky and became even more distressed.

Darwin wasn't sure what to do. Even though the dinosaur was crying pitifully, he'd never heard of a therizinosaurus before. He looked every bit like a carnivore and Darwin didn't entirely trust him.

Dippy Egg wasn't so cautious. Without hesitating, he picked up the soggy hanky, wrung it out and dabbed gently at the beast's dripping nostrils. Unpleasant as it was, it wasn't nearly as stomach churning as cleaning Flint's toenails.

'Cheer up, matey,' said Dippy. 'It might never happen.'

'But it *has* already happened!' wailed the therizinosaurus and, with great gulps and sobs, it swung its massive legs out from under the sheets, revealing a dragon-like tail.

Thinking he was about to show his true colours and pounce, Darwin leapt sideways and hid. Unfortunately, this hurt his feelings enormously and he started sobbing all over again.

'Why does everyone hate me?' he wailed, as Darwin stood up again. 'I know I look like a vicious flesh-ripping theropod,' he said, gazing

mournfully at the metre-long claws on his scaly hands, 'but I'm not a carnivore – I'm a harmless omnivore. Honestly, I am.'

'I believe you,' said Dippy, who was a harmless omnivore too. 'I hate meat. I like eggs though.'

The therizinosaurus smiled through his tears. 'You do? Me too – I *love* eggs!'

'I'll cook you some,' said Uncle Loops. 'You must be starving. How do you like them, boiled or strangled?'

The strange new dinosaur looked thoughtful. 'Boiled, please,' he said politely, 'but not too runny if you don't mind. I once had a runny egg with a snotty chick on a string inside it and I'm afraid I threw up.'

'I hate it when that chick thing happens,' agreed Dippy.

As Darwin looked at the gallimimus and the therizinosaurus chatting away together, he could see why they were bonding. They looked rather similar – they were almost the same height and shape. Dippy's beak was longer and his claws weren't nearly as spectacular, but that might have been because he bit his nails – he'd had plenty to be nervous about living with Flint.

'Eggs up!' announced Uncle Loops a few minutes later, arriving with a tray. 'The hard-boiled one is for you with the big claws. Sorry, I've forgotten your name, pal. I'm Uncle Poops, by the way.'

'It's Loops,' whispered Darwin discreetly. 'I'm Darwin and this is Dippy.'

'Pleased to meet you, Darwin, Dippy, Uncle Ploops,' said the therizinosaurus. 'I'm Graham.'

'Graham? I won't forget that in a hurry,' said the ancient stegosaurus. 'So tell me, Gary, what brings you to Fossil Street?'

Neatly biffing the top off his egg, Graham told them his sorry tale. He had stowed away on a boat from Mongolia with his parents to start a new life in Uptown, but his father's sat-nav went horribly wrong and they got lost Downtown in Raptor Road. Sadly, they were found by a two-tonne megalosaurus on a night out with his friends. The meat market had run out of kebabs, so they'd had a therizinosaurus take-away instead.

'Somehow I escaped,' continued Graham, 'but they took poor Mummy and Daddy away and made mincemeat out of them.'

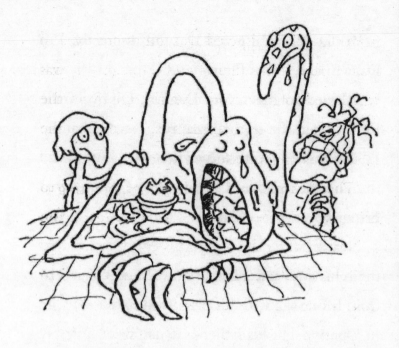

He banged his head on his yolky plate in grief and wailed, 'Those carnivores ate my parents! I'm an *orphhhhhhan!*'

Darwin patted him on the shoulder until he stopped shuddering. 'Let it all out, Graham. I know how you feel,' he said. 'Those carnivores ate my brother, Livingstone. What's more, they're going to eat my parents if I don't rescue them from the Primeval Forest as soon as possible.'

'It's scary out there,' said Graham. 'I was wandering round on my own for days. I saw the most hideous creature scuttling round in the bushes pushing a trolley on wheels.'

'That was me,' said Uncle Loops, pointing to his zimmer frame. 'I was looking for my cap. You didn't happen to see it, did you?'

Graham thought back. 'Well, now I come to think of it, I did see a rather theatrical —'

'Knitted cap?' said Loops hopefully.

Graham shook his head. 'No, a rather theatrical triceratops. He was swinging a cane and singing a tune from *Hairy Poppins*, but when I said hello, he screamed and ran away.'

Darwin grinned knowingly. 'That was Sir Stratford Tempest. After he saw you, he went running to Boris the mayor and spread rumours that you were a ferocious carnivore. Flint

Beastwood thinks you want to take over his territory and has vowed to hunt you down.'

'Me? Ferocious?' quivered the therizinosaurus. 'I wouldn't hurt a fly.'

'Beastwood don't know that, though, does he?' said Dippy. 'I wouldn't want to be in your shoes, mate. He tried to hunt me down too but Darwin tricked him into attacking a stuffed carnival costume instead and —'

'Aha!' whooped Darwin excitedly. 'Costumes! We've fooled Flint once – we can fool him again. I've just thought of a brilliant way to rescue Mum and Dad. All we need to do is . . .'

He looked at the orphaned therizinosaurus and trailed off.

'Why are you staring at me?' asked Graham. 'Do I have egg on my beak?'

'No, no,' said Darwin reluctantly. 'Nothing like that.'

He'd just realised that he could only make the plan work if Graham did something extremely brave and daring, but it didn't seem fair to ask him.

'I can only do it with your help, Graham,' he admitted, 'but you've been through far too much already. I can't ask you. It's too dangerous.'

Graham flicked a bit of egg shell off his impressive pectoral muscles. 'That's a bit harsh, Darwin,' he said. 'I may be an emotional wreck right now but I'm not a coward. I know what it is like to have both parents eaten. After all your kindness, the least I can do is help you save yours.'

'Good for you, Gordon!' said Uncle Loops. 'Let him help if he wants to, Tarquin. You two can go off and save Horace and Linda and I'll look after young Dopey here.'

'It's Maurice and Lydia, and he's Dippy,' Darwin reminded him quietly, pointing at the gallimimus.

'I did think he had a screw loose,' agreed Uncle Loops. Darwin scribbled down a list of things he required for his master plan and read them out. 'I need paint, scissors, cardboard, glue and that moth-eaten mammoth fur coat that's stinking out your wardrobe, Uncle.'

'Very well,' said Uncle Loops, 'but look after it – I hear vintage is back in fashion.'

'Mammoth fur went out in the Meiocene,' said Darwin. 'Graham, can you act?'

'I know my Shake Spear,' said the therizinosaurus. '*Out, damned spot! Out, out I say! Will these claws ne'er be clean?* That's a line from Lardy Macbeth's speech.'

'Fantastic!' said Darwin. 'If anything, you're overqualified. I only need you to roar.'

After gathering the items on Darwin's list, and a little preparation, the stage was set. They smiled at each other.

'With acting skills like Graham's, how could this plan possibly fail?' said Darwin.

'Let me count the ways . . .' mumbled Uncle Loops.

CHAPTER 9
TRULY A-MAZE-ING

Down in the deep, dark Primeval Forest, something stirred. Was it *homo erectus* finding his feet? Was it a recently discovered species of megapotamus playing hopscotch with his chums? No, it was Sir Tempest doing his utmost to hold back an almighty sneeze.

Still heavily disguised as a tree, he was butt to butt with Mrs Merrick who was head to head with Mr Stigson in a circle of Uptown herbivores trying to pass themselves off as a maze to corner the Downtown carnivores and prevent them from leaving.

So far, it had worked. Under Mr Stigson's leadership, they had crept through the brambly shortcut and got ahead of Flint Beastwood's gang and trapped them.

It would have been a lot harder to achieve if it hadn't had been misty, and their enemies hadn't been arguing, but Terry O'Dactyl was winding up Mr Cretaceous to the point of insanity, Liz Vicious was having a terrific ding-dong with Flint and as none of them was concentrating, they blundered straight into the mock maze.

'Holy moley, mother of clod!' panicked the pteranodon. 'Where's the exit, Boss? It used to be

150

right here. I can't see the wood for the trees . . .
Argh, that one moved, so it did!'

Flint Beastwood slapped his beak.

'Ow!' shrieked Terry. 'Why would you do that
to me, Boss?'

'Icy calm, Mr O'Dactyl,' muttered Flint. 'You
have wings, do you not? With a view from
above, you will be able to guide us out.'

'He won't, Boss,' grumbled the deinosuchus,
trying to squeeze hopelessly between the part of

the maze that was Mrs Merrick and Sir Tempest.

'He will if I tell him to!' insisted Beastwood. 'O'Dactyl? Fly into the sky immediately and get us out of here or I'll rip your wings off and fry them Southern style.'

The gibbering pteranodon made a feeble attempt to launch himself, but as the fake trees were so close together, he couldn't get a decent run-up.

'You've got the flight skills of a sack of spuds!' roared Beastwood. 'Try harder!'

'The runway's too short for him to take off,' explained Mr Cretaceous, grabbing Terry by the neck. 'Want me to launch him, Boss?'

'It's worth a try,' said Flint, and the deinosuchus flung the miserable

pteranodon
into the
air.

O'Dactyl
lingered
for a few seconds then
crashed back down to earth and lay on
his back like a foul, broken kite.

'Is the exit to the left or to the right?' demanded Flint.

'Couldn't see, had my eyes shut,' squealed Terry, scuttling away from Flint and wedging himself against Sir Tempest's feet which were cunningly disguised as roots.

It was at that point that the Stratford sneeze started to build. Whether it was caused by a dangling cherry or one of Mrs Merrick's tail hairs tickling his nostrils, he couldn't tell. He hoped it was the cherry, but whatever had caused the dreadful itch, it wasn't going away.

Protruding his lower lip, he tried to direct a sharp breath up his left nostril to blast the irritating thing away but all it did was make it vibrate in an even more ticklish, toe-curling manner. Holding his breath didn't help – it just made him feel giddy, and falling over like a piece of rotten timber was not an option – the carnivores would immediately escape through the gap.

With his left hand on Ernest's shoulder and his right hand on Frank's, he was unable to scratch himself without breaking the carefully formed arch. Finally, his lungs inflated like blimps at an airshow, and the sneeze burst out with the ferocity of a nuclear explosion.

The shockwave rendered the carnivores silent for a few seconds but, as the maze collapsed in a soggy heap of twigs and tantrums, the Uptown herbivores were exposed.

Flint Beastwood's eyes glowed like hot coals as Mr Stigson tried to explain.

'We're going to a fancy dress party as an Enchanted Forest.' He grinned feebly.

'It's cancelled, Maurice,' replied Beastwood as he tied the herbivores tightly together with a stout rope. 'Shall I tell you where you're going?'

'Yes, please, Mr Beastwood,' lied Mr Stigson as

the tyrannosaurus circled him, pulling bits of
foliage off his disguise.

'You are going nowhere,' said Beastwood. 'Oh
look, your leaves are falling. It must be autumn.
I love autumn, don't you, Maurice?'

'Yes!' said Mr Stigson gaily. 'Season of mists
and mellow fruitfulness . . .'

'Autumn is all those things and more,' mused
Flint poetically. ''Tis the season for all herbivores

who have made a maze of themselves to be slaughtered on the spot.'

Mr Cretaceous gnashed his teeth and balled his cabbage-sized fists. 'Want me to slaughter them now, Boss?' he drooled.

'Don't be greedy, Mr Cretaceous,' said Flint, twirling an imaginary moustache like a pantomime villain. 'Why should you have all the fun? We're *all* going to slaughter them!'

'Oh no you can't!' wailed Mrs Stigson.

'Oh yes we can!' laughed Flint nastily. 'And then we're going round to your house to teach that son of yours a lesson.'

'I've heard that vinegar is good for getting blood out of carpets,' snickered Liz Vicious as she spat on her claws and prepared to attack.

'On the count of three, kill!' commanded Beastwood as the herbivores clung to each other and said their last goodbyes.

'Farewell, old thing. I've always fancied you, Sir Tempest,' said Mrs Merrick.

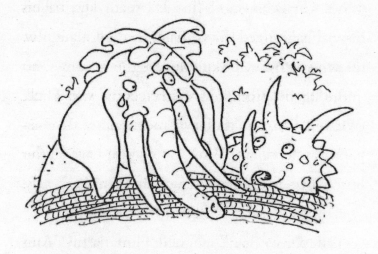

'One!' growled Beastwood.

'Goodbye, Phyllis,' said Tempest fondly. 'I've always fancied you, Maurice.'

'Two!' roared Beastwood. 'Two and a half . . . thr—'

Just as the carnivores were about to commit carnage, Terry O'Dactyl started flapping up and down and pointing into the distance.

'Look, Boss! There's Dippy, so he is!'

Knowing the pteranodon was too deranged to be a liar, Beastwood turned and, adjusting his piggy eyes into sharp focus, he let out a low, drawn-out growl. Skulking in the shadows, no more than a hundred metres away, was a tall, stooped figure with gangly legs and a familiar-looking beak carrying a pair of suitcases. Whoever it was kept looking over their shoulder nervously, as if they was afraid someone was after them.

'It's him, Beastie!' whispered Liz Vicious urgently.

Flint thrashed his tail like a saber-toothed tiger about to pounce on its prey.

'Dippy Egg, you skanky bit of dripping!' he hissed. 'Come to Daddy!'

As the deadly tyrannosaurus and his gang raced off after him, the herbivores drew a collective sigh of relief.

'Thank goodness for that. Now we can all go home,' said Mrs Merrick. 'Forget what I said earlier about my feelings for you and untie me, Sir Tempest.'

'I'm an actor, dear, not a sailor,' he said. 'I don't know a reef knot from a granny. I could try rubbing against your binding with my horn,' huffed the triceratops, 'but after you took back what you said earlier, you can wait. I'm going to help Maurice first.'

Mr Stigson had been wriggling, but it was no good, it was just making the rope tighter. 'Are you sure you haven't got any scissors in your handbag, Lydia?' he asked for the tenth time. 'Heaven knows you keep everything else in there.'

'It doesn't matter how many times you ask, I still have no scissors,' insisted Mrs Stigson. 'I don't want to be stuck here forever any more than you do. Let's scream for help.'

'No,' said Mr Stigson, 'it's girlish. Anyway, what's the point? No one will hear us.'

'You've never heard me scream, have you Maurice?' said Sir Tempest. 'I'm highly trained, I've been in horror films. You should have heard me in *Jack the Kipper* – I was that loud, they heard me screaming in Hollywood. Allow me to demonstrate: '**HEEEEEEEEEEEELP!**'

If the Uptown herbivores had been able to release their hands they would have clapped them over their ears. While they were almost deafened, Sir Tempest's scream seemed to do the trick — the bushes began to rustle. Someone out there had heard them.

'Hooray!' cried Mrs Merrick. 'It's our saviour!'

'Boo!' cried everyone else miserably. 'It's the australopithecus!'

Standing before them brandishing his axe was the hairy, scruffy sub-human who had tried to chop them down for firewood — or was it?

'He does look skuzzy but izzy Ozzi?' mused Sir Tempest.

Unusually, Nogs wasn't with him, he'd lost his limp and he seemed to have grown somehow.

'I expect he's grown from stealing our food, that's why!' groaned Mrs Merrick. 'Either that or it's Ozzi's father. Get away from me, you filthy

little ape. Your chest hair needs a trim.'

'It's only me!' said a voice, removing the wild
wig he was wearing for a moment. 'I disguised
myself as Ozzi to get past Mr Beastwood and
rescue you. It's not real chest hair, it's snippings
from Uncle Loops's mammoth fur coat.'

'Darwin!' wept Mrs Stigson. 'We've been so
worried about you.'

'I'm fine,' said Darwin, slicing through the
rope with his axe and freeing his family and
neighbours.

'You should never have defied Boris's curfew,'

scolded Mr Stigson. 'From what I hear, you played a very risky trick on Flint Beastwood – something about a dragon costume?'

Mrs Stigson dug her husband in the ribs. 'Not now, Maurice. Darwin just saved our lives.'

'Yes he did and he's my little hero!' said Mrs Merrick, giving him a sloppy kiss. 'Did he think to bring any sweets or sandwiches, I wonder?'

Darwin shook his head. 'I was in a bit of a rush.'

'You selfish little beggar,' muttered the mastodon, and turned her back on him.

Mrs Stigson flung her arms around her son and gave him a good squeeze. But her joy at seeing him safe and sound was short-lived as she remembered Dippy. He was running for his life and might even be dead, or even worse – enslaved. How could she break the awful news to Darwin?

'What's up, Mum? 'he asked.

'I hate to tell you this, son,' she said, 'but a little while ago, the carnivores saw your friend, Dippy, in the woods carrying his suitcases and I'm afraid they chased after him and . . .'

Mrs Stigson was so upset she couldn't finish the sentence but to her surprise, Darwin was smiling a huge smile.

'Don't worry. Dippy will be miles away by now. I'll prove it – follow me!'

CHAPTER 10

MASTER OF DISGUISE

Keen as the Uptown Dinosaurs were to follow
Darwin and discover the fate of the gallimimus,
they had been tied up for so long, some of them
were in desperate need of a wee – at least, Mrs
Merrick was.

'Can't you hang on, Phyllis?' asked Mrs

Stigson discreetly. 'We need to set off.'

Mrs Merrick crossed her legs and frowned. 'Lydia, I'd like to see you hang on after you'd drunk a small pond,' she grunted. 'Excuse me while I sneak behind that tree and do my business – no peeking anyone!'

She rushed off and while the rest of the neighbours tried not to listen to what sounded like a water tank bursting, the tree she was crouched behind suddenly leapt back, danced up and down and waved its branches in the air frantically.

'Eughhh . . . Of all the trees in all the woods, why choose me, Phyllis?' it wailed, exposing Mrs Merrick in mid-flow.

'I'm sorry, Sir Tempest,' she said, blushing to the tip of her trunk. 'It's your own silly fault for wearing such a convincing disguise.'

It was all too hilarious for the ankylosaurs

who were clutching their sides and rocking with laughter.

'Grow up, you silly boys!' snapped Mrs Merrick, shaking her tail. 'Lead on, Darwin, what are we waiting for?'

The residents of Fossil Street followed behind the little stegosaurus and did their best to stop giggling at Mrs Merrick. As they went deeper and deeper into the wilderness, Mr Stigson started to panic.

'Are we nearly there yet, Darwin? Only we've been going round in circles for rather a long time. There's no shame in admitting you're lost, son.'

Mrs Stigson tutted softly. 'Don't humiliate him, Maurice. You never admit it when you're lost.'

Darwin marched on confidently. 'I'm not lost,' he said, chopping through a fence of wicked brambles with his axe. 'We're nearly there . . . mind the thorns, Mum.'

'Ow! That prickle nearly had my eye out!' boomed Sir Tempest. 'Luckily, I have an eye-patch at home from when I played Captain Slack Marrow in *Pachyderms of the Caribbean*. My agent said Jerry Deep wasn't a patch on me and —'

Darwin held his hand up and the collection of bedraggled trees and foliage stopped walking.

'We're here,' he said, pointing to a cave. 'It's

the same one I hid in when I was on the run from Beastwood – it's where I found Dippy.'

'Is he in there now?' whispered Mrs Stigson.

Darwin was about to answer when he heard the dreaded sound of pounding of footsteps in the near distance, followed by a distinctive war cry.

'Just you wait till I catch you, you great long streak of yolk!' roared Beastwood.

The scales stood up on the back of Darwin's neck. 'The Downtown carnivores are coming back this way! Quick everybody, arrange yourselves in a forest-like manner behind those thick vines hanging either side of the cave.'

The Uptown dinosaurs didn't need telling twice and almost fell over themselves in the unseemly scramble to secure the best hiding place.

Seconds later, they all watched in dread as a

terrified figure that looked awfully like Dippy came charging through the undergrowth and ran straight past them into the cave. He'd just made it inside when Beastwood burst onto the scene, flanked by Mr Cretaceous, Liz Vicious and Terry O'Dactyl.

'I know where Dippy is, Boss!' squeaked the pteranodon, skittering in sickening circles in front of the cave. 'He's in there, so he is!'

'Thank you, Terry,' said Flint Beastwood as he unwittingly leant on Mrs Merrick's buttocks to catch his breath. 'We all know where he is, that's the beauty of it.'

'Can we kill him now . . . please?' wheedled the deinosuchus.

The tyrannosaurus stroked his chin and paced up and down teasingly as he considered it. 'Kill him, Mr Cretaceous? No, no, no. I need a slave to give me a full pedicure after all this chasing about. I've trodden in all sorts – do my feet smell a bit iffy to you, Elizabeth?'

He lifted his foot up for the velociraptor to sniff.

'Very iffy, Beastie,' she gagged. 'It's a blend of cynognathus muck and old fossils, with a hint of mastodon wee.'

Mr Cretaceous folded his arms and sighed. 'So you want me to drag him out alive?' he said, unable to hide his disappointment.

Flint smiled a crooked smile. '*Barely* alive, please, Mr C.'

The deinosuchus beamed with delight, rolled up his imaginary sleeves and began to strut his way into the cave, closely followed by the others.

Darwin could feel his mother shaking with fright in front of him. 'Oh, poor Dippy!' she sobbed. 'I can't bear to look!'

'Mum, he'll be fine, I promise,' whispered Darwin. 'You'll see.'

'We're coming to get you, Dipstick!' bellowed Beastwood.

The Uptown herbivores listened to the

carnivores cursing and calling as they searched
the cave.

Suddenly there was a ghastly silence.

'Oh noooo . . . they must have found him,'
squeaked Mrs Stigson.

There was a blood-curdling roar, as the creature they thought was Dippy reared up to its full height and dropped the suitcases to reveal its terrifying, metre-long claws. Snapping the elastic

on its harmless-looking cardboard beak disguise, it revealed its real one, which looked as sharp and as deadly as a giant pair of secateurs.

'Get away from me, you brute!' cowered Flint.

'Please don't eat me – I'll give you anything you want . . . my food . . . my empire . . . I'll even throw in Elizabeth.'

'Go, Graham!' laughed Darwin, throwing his Ozzi wig up in the air triumphantly as the therizinosaurus chased Beastwood and his gang out of the cave and through the forest.

'It's safe to come out now, everybody,' said Darwin. 'I don't think we'll be seeing Mr Beastwood for a while.'

'Who the heck is Graham?' asked Mr Stigson.

'Oh, he's just a friend,' said Darwin. 'He's been sleeping in Uncle Loops's bed.'

'*What?*' wailed Mrs Stigson. 'I wish I'd known – I'd have changed the linen.'

Quickly getting over the embarrassment of having a guest see Augustus's filthy bottom sheet, she remembered Dippy. 'But if Dippy isn't in the cave, where has he gone?'

'Well, he was at our house,' explained Darwin as they set off for home, 'but hopefully he'll be on a ship halfway to America by now. I asked Uncle Loops to take him down to the docks.'

Mr Stigson looked concerned, removing his tree disguise as the rest of his neighbours did the same. 'Hmm, that sounds risky. The docks are close to carnivore territory – any one of them might have recognised Dippy and recaptured him as a favour to Beastwood.'

'No one would have recognised him,' said Darwin, smiling. 'Not even his own mother, if she was still alive, poor thing. I left Uncle Loops to disguise him as a carnival queen.'

Sir Tempest Stratford perked up immediately. 'I'm sorry I missed that!' he declared. 'I played a queen once, you know.'

'Just the once?' muttered Mrs Merrick. 'I find that rather hard to believe.'

As the weary band of herbivores made their way across No Man's Land back to Fossil Street, Mr Stigson thanked the neighbours for their help and invited them in for drinks.

'It's not us you have to thank, dear boy,' said Sir Tempest, 'it's young Darwin who saved the day. He really is a master of disguise!'

But, as it turned out, Darwin wasn't the only

one. When the Stigsons went inside, they were confronted by a rare and unusual sight. There, sitting rather awkwardly on the couch, was a carnival queen with the proportions of a gallimimus but the appearance of a very large lady wearing a curly wig, a skirt with a frilly petticoat, a pair of thigh boots and a blouse stuffed with a pair of honeydew melons.

'I was going to use those in a salad!' gasped Mrs Stigson.

'Well, *hello!*' said Sir Tempest, fruitily.

'Oh, Dippy, what has my uncle done to you?' squeaked Darwin.

But that wasn't the worst of it – sitting on the carnival queen's lap, with his arm draped lovingly round her shoulder, was a character so hairy and scruffy, it looked as if someone had snipped fur from an old coat and stuck them all over his body.

'Please tell me that's another one of your disguises, Darwin,' said Mrs Merrick.

It wasn't.

'It's the australopithecus,' said Uncle Loops, leaning casually on his zimmer frame. 'What can

I say? The poor creature has fallen in love with Dippy's disguise.'

As if to prove the point, Ozzi produced a bouquet of dandelions and a sparkly ring out of his duffel bag and, getting down on one woolly

knee, he said four little grunts to Dippy which could only have meant one thing – they were engaged. As Ozzi clutched at his little sub-human heart and gazed longingly into Dippy's eyes, even Nogs was welling up.

'Call me an old romantic, but I didn't have the heart to tell him,' said Uncle Loops.

The Uptown and Downtown Prehistoric Spotter's Guide

Dinosaurs

Stegosaurus

(Steg-oh-saw-rus)

Example: The Stigsons

Triceratops

(Try-sair-a-tops)

Example: Sir Tempest

Edmontonia

(Ed-mon-toe-nee-a)

Example: Boris the mayor

Ankylosaur

(Ank-ee-lo-saw)

Example: Frank
and Ernest

Mamenchisaurus

(Mah-men-chee-saw-rus)

Example: Lou Gooby

Tyrannosaurus rex

(Tie-ran-o-saw-rus rex)

Example: Flint Beastwood

Velociraptor

(Veh-loss-i-rap-tor)

Example: Liz Vicious

Gallimimus

(Gall-uh-my-mus)

Example: Dippy Egg

Therizinosaurus

(There-ah-zino-saw-rus)

Example: Graham

OTHER PREHISTORIC CREATURES

Deinosuchus

(Day-no-sook-us)

Example: Mr Cretaceous

Pteranodon

(Tehr-ran-oh-don)

Example: Terry

O'Dactyl

Mastodon

(Mas-toe-don)

Example: Mrs Merrick

Australopithecus

(Oss-tra-lo-pith-ah-cus)

Example: Ozzi

Cynognathus

(Sigh-nog-nay-thus)

Example: Nogs

**DISCOVER THE
DOWNTOWN DINOSAURS
ONLINE!**

DOWNTOWNDINOSAURS.CO.UK

**GAMES
PUZZLES
FACT-FILES
AND MORE!**